Dethroning Oz
Twisted Tales of Familiar Faces
Audrey Brice

M4L Publishing

To all those who willingly stand up and fight against tyranny.

Tornado

Toto let out two loud barks that descended into a low growl. Glancing over, I examined the curtain-covered window next to the front door, expecting to see a shadow. It would have been strange if there had been one. It was past six in the evening. Deep Creek, Kansas, was remote, hidden deep among the prairie in the middle of nowhere. The outside world even had it listed as a dead town. Nature had reclaimed the town center, miles away from me, in a mess of prairie plants and weeds. There was a single road off the main interstate that led to this small house, and it wasn't well-marked. Few people visited save for the occasional family member or my boyfriend, Mark, who lived in Topeka and came out for a few weekends each month.

My black German shepherd, Toto, growled again. Glancing at the boiling pot on the stove, I turned down the heat, wiped my hands on a tea towel, and went to the door. Pulling back the curtain, I looked onto the front porch. Nothing. "There's no one here, silly," I told him.

Toto let out a disgruntled half-bark, half-growl, cocked his head to one side and just looked at me. I rarely locked the door since I was so far out, but before I went back to the kitchen, I turned the deadbolt, just in case. I wasn't an idiot. This small house wasn't much in the way of size, but it was perfect for just one person. I'd inherited it from my Great Aunt Em, who'd died just outside the house from a heart attack at seventy-four. It was a cousin who'd found her—two weeks after the fact. When no one in the family wanted the house, worried her unquiet spirit would haunt them, I offered to buy out my cousins' shares and the seventy-five acres of farmland the house sat on. I leased most of the property to big agra. It paid the mortgage. I liked the solitude. Here, I could whip up my potions late into the night, grow my own herbs and vegetables, and wildcraft everything for my online shop, which is how I made my real living. Luckily, the house ran off of solar, had a well, and a leach field. I also had three generators, just in case, alongside the satellite Internet service installed when I'd moved in.

Once or twice a month, I went into the nearby city of Manhattan, twenty miles southeast, and Toto and I would make a day of it. Not once since I'd moved in had Aunt Em's ghost haunted me. That's not to say she didn't occasionally show up for a chat, but Toto didn't growl at her. He'd known Aunt Em when he was a puppy, and they had gotten along well when she was alive. They got along well now that she was in the spirit world, too.

I went back to the kitchen to work on the veil-parting potion, leaving Toto to guard us from imaginary threats by staring at the closed door and the empty yard beyond. While I recited the spell and made magic gestures over the potion, the wind outside picked up, causing the trees to sway. Toto scrambled to his feet and barked, and a chill ran through me. The hair on my arms stood on end, as if electrified by something intangible in the air. Outside, the roar of the wind intensified.

"Shit. Tornado!" I ran toward Toto, pulling him along with me. "Come on." Together, we raced into the inner bathroom. With the dog in my arms, I settled into the bathtub, holding him close. There was no way we could get to the root cellar in the backyard in time, as the house didn't have a basement. The bathroom tub would have to do. Tremors rattled the house. Toto whimpered in my arms. Drawing in a deep breath, I began reciting a warding spell, hoping it would offer us some protection.

Mark had told me he didn't like me living out here alone. He'd warned me to keep a radio on because there were no tornado sirens this far out in the middle of nowhere. Next summer, we'd planned to build a new house, one with a basement that could serve as a tornado shelter. The only reason we were waiting was because his contract job didn't end until the coming April.

A loud crash, followed by the sound of shattering glass, made me double down on the spell, visualizing a protective bubble around Toto and me. The entire house trembled and shook. It was so loud that I tried to drown it out with my voice by screaming my protection chant and calling on the storm gods to keep us safe. Suddenly, everything went silent, and the wind stopped, but my senses still reverberated with energy. Something wasn't right. The entire room jolted as if something had picked the house up, off its foundation, and dropped it. Then everything went still. Toto trembled next to me, and I did the same. We sat there for a few minutes. When nothing else happened, I lifted my head and looked around. Everything that had been in the bathroom cupboards was now strewn all over the floor, and the room seemed tilted a bit, as if the house was now uneven.

"Shit," I whispered. The tornado had actually moved the house. Which meant the house would be unlivable until next spring, and I'd be forced to move back to Topeka. I'd have to find a short-term rental that allowed dogs. Climbing out of the bathtub, I carefully made my way to the door with Toto at my heels. The door swung open easily, revealing the hallway that led to the living room and kitchen, and to my bedroom. My life's possessions lay scattered everywhere. "Damn it."

Maybe I could borrow or rent an RV, I thought, then frowned at the idea. "Damn it," I said again, briefly mourning all the store inventory I'd likely lost. Luckily, I'd filled and sent the orders I had the day before, so whatever orders came in today could be easily dealt with by emailing the customer to let them know my situation. Toto rushed past me to the front door. He wanted to be out on solid ground, and I didn't blame him. So did I. I scanned what remained of the living room and kitchen for my cell phone but couldn't find it among the disaster. I'd have to look for it later, I decided. In the meantime, we needed to get out of the house so I could assess the damage and see if we were still in danger, in which case we would hurry to the root cellar in the back. From the sunlight coming in through the holes in the roof and the broken windows, that didn't seem to be the case though. Opening the front door, my heart almost stopped. The view outside had completely transformed from the flat prairies of Deep Creek, Kansas, to a lush landscape with rolling hills and forests of trees not far away.

Beside me, Toto took in our surroundings, sniffed at the fragrant air, and then looked up at me, his eyes just as confused as mine. "What the hell?" I whispered under my breath. "I don't think we're in Kansas anymore," I said.

Toto carefully stepped out onto the moderately damaged porch and down the steps to sniff at the grass around the house. He glanced up at me as if to ask if I was following, but I felt frozen, unsure whether I wanted to know exactly where we'd ended up. It was when Toto disappeared around the side of the house and began barking frantically that I could coax my legs forward to follow him.

As I rounded the corner, my hand went to my mouth when I saw what all the fuss was about. Sticking out from under my house were a pair of women's legs. On her feet was a very fancy pair of glittery silver-and-red stilettos. A bit of blood stained her legs just where the edge of the house was. Presumably the rest of her lay pinned and crushed under the house. She was dead. *Fuck*, my mind screamed.

I pulled my hand from my mouth and took a deep breath. "Okay. Don't panic, it's not like it's your fault the house fell on someone. The townspeople won't come after you with torches and pitchforks. This was just a freak storm and a freak accident," I said aloud. My voice was reassuring, and hearing it made Toto stop barking, too.

Toto looked at me expectantly. I gave him a nod. "We find help. That's what we do. We'll just start walking and look for a town, or a farm..." I turned and started toward the front of the house. "Come on, Toto."

He followed.

We didn't even make it to what appeared to be a road when we saw people coming toward us. Some with orange hair, others with green, and weirdly, they all wore the same shade of pale blue. Now, orange and green hair were nothing shocking. Not to me, anyway. I'd attended the witch fairs and conventions where everyone had their own style, various hair colors, piercings of all types, and tattoos. But these people almost looked like they were in some kind of cult. Toto growled, so I reached down and took him by the collar, wishing I had a leash. There probably was one somewhere in the house.

Then I heard the roar of an engine in the distance and from over the hill in the other direction, a silver motorcycle appeared. On it, a figure dressed in brilliant bright white.

"Good gods. Leave it to me to end up in some creepy small town with a dead body beneath my house," I mumbled under my breath, then threw on an awkward half-smile. "Uh, hi! I apparently got caught up in a tornado," I told the approaching group of people in blue. The motorcycle didn't stop; just kept on going past us as if nothing was out of the ordinary.

A man with a green pornstache was the first to reach me. He gave me a nod. "Who are ya now?"

"I'm Dorothy Gale from Deep Creek," I replied, wondering if I should shake his hand.

"What now?" He squinted his eyes at me and frowned as the remaining seven people came to a stop behind him. Apparently, he was the leader.

"I'm Dorothy from Deep Creek," I repeated.

"Weird name," he said. "And where's this Deep Creek?"

"Twenty miles Southeast of Manhattan," I said. "Manhattan, Kansas," I clarified, because the man's face still bore a mask of confusion.

He shook his head. "There's no Deep Creek, Manhattan, or Kansas anywhere around here." Then he turned to the other onlookers. "Any of you ever heard of those places?"

They all shook their heads.

Country bumpkins. A cult of country bumpkins, I thought. "Can you tell me where I am?" Clearly, it made more sense for me to find out where I was rather than having to explain where I came from.

"Of course," Green Pornstache said. "You're in the Land of Oz."

I felt my eyes widen, unbidden. Where the fuck was Oz? Then a sense of dread and horror washed over me. The potion. My hand went to my mouth. I'd been in the middle of making a veil-parting potion when the tornado came. Something must have gone wrong. It looked like a portal had opened, and we were pushed right through it. *Shit.*

"Look!" cried one woman with bright orange spiky hair and a high shrieky voice, pointing to the flashy stilettos poking out from under my house. The cult gasped.

"You killed her," Green Pornstache said in disbelief.

"I didn't mean to. I mean, I didn't do it," I said quickly. "There was a tornado, and next thing I knew I was here and..." I held onto Toto and wondered how the hell I was going to get Toto and myself back to Kansas. Maybe with the house. Maybe not.

But then, Green Pornstache put on a great big smile and in a relieved voice said, "That nasty old witch is finally dead."

The others behind him perked up too. Except for the orange spiky-haired woman. "Now you have to worry about Janice."

"Who's Janice?" I'd worked with a Janice once. She was the head of HR and no one liked her. It appeared that here, too, no one liked Janice.

"She was Gertrude's sister," the woman said with a nod. She looked strange. Aside from the wild orange spiky hair, she had an oddly pointed chin, big brown eyes, and a small, flat nose.

I brushed off her strangeness. "Who's Gertrude?" I asked.

All eight of them pointed to the person lying dead under my house. Now that she had a name, it all seemed more real. Would Janice sue me? Try to get me for manslaughter? I shook off my brief bout of paranoia. It was an accident. A freak storm combined with freak magic. No one would dare try to say I did it on purpose.

"They're wicked witches," Green Pornstache told me matter-of-factly. "The wickedest witches in Oz."

This information surprised me. Surely, if there were witches here, one of two things would happen. The first is that they'd understand it was an accident. Or second, they'd curse me. I frowned. "Well, when will the authorities arrive then? Clearly, we need to file a police report."

I was met with blank stares.

I drew in a deep breath and pursed my lips. "I'm going to go get a leash for Toto and grab a few things." There was nothing left to do but go back into the house, grab Toto's leash, find my cell phone, and pack a few sundries, including my grimoire. Then, I'd have to find out if my phone still worked and contact the police myself. Maybe find a dog-friendly hotel.

Leaving the cult gawking at my house and the body beneath it, I carefully went back inside and began collecting everything I needed.

The Tin Woodsman

I EMERGED WITH TOTO on his leash and a small magical pack that had more room on the inside than looked possible from the outside, filled to the brim with my laptop, granola bars for me, a few plastic bags of dog food and treats, three changes of clothes, a first aid kit, a lighter, a flashlight, a small blanket, my grimoire, and a pen and paper. My phone, which was only a month old, had survived the tornado and still had a full charge, but no signal. Go figure.

Some cultists had gone back to wherever they came from, but Pornstache and Spiky-haired Lady were still there. "What are your names?" I asked, knowing I'd need to know them.

"Robert," Pornstache said.

"Lisa," Spiky-haired Lady said.

I made a note on my phone. "And your phone numbers?"

More blank stares. Did these people not know what a phone was? *Not if you slipped through some kind of portal*, my mind silently chastised me.

"How do I contact you if I need witnesses?" When met with more questioning looks, I steeled my temper. "Where do you live?"

"In a small village beyond those trees and the hedgerow over there," Robert said, pointing at a border of wild shrubs that met up with a copse of trees. It looked more like a thicket due to the dense underbrush. I could see nothing beyond the thicket because the landscape dropped away into what I assumed must have been a gentle sloping valley.

I realized then that I likely would not get any real answers to my questions, but I had a few more anyway. "And who would I contact to report this incident and maybe get back home?"

"Oh, well, the Wizard." The man nodded as if this was the most obvious answer.

Lisa nodded in agreement. "Yes, he'll know what to do."

I perked up. Finally—a real answer. "Where can I find this wizard?"

"Follow the road," Robert said, pointing to the cobbled, yellow-colored road. "Follow it until you reach the Emerald City." He pointed and my eyes followed. In the distance, I could barely make out a spire from a church or maybe a skyscraper.

"Well, thank the gods for that," I muttered. The promise of a city with hotels and a hot shower—and hopefully normal people—filled me with hope. Maybe I could get a cell signal there, too. "You remember my name, right?"

Robert gave a single nod with his green head of hair. "Yes. Dorothy."

"Right," I said. "I guess I'm off to see your wizard. If anyone asks, I'll be making my way to the Emerald City."

I turned, with Toto leading the way, and started down the yellow cobblestone road toward civilization.

We'd walked maybe half a mile, and the verdant hill my house had landed on was out of sight. The path ahead darkened with shade from the tall standing trees on either side of the road. The forest became denser here, with thick underbrush and air redolent with pine and earth. I paid attention to the plants, trying to identify them for potions and other witchy brews, but I didn't recognize any of them. Glancing at my phone, there still wasn't a signal, so I slid it into my back jeans pocket and kept moving.

A half hour later, Toto stopped dead in his tracks and turned to the right. We hadn't encountered anyone on the road, which was strange in itself, and I was ready with a spell, just in case someone tried to rob us.

"Mmmm," came a muffled voice, almost like someone had been gagged. Not that I knew firsthand what a gagged person sounded like, but I watched television like everyone else. That was definitely a gagged noise.

"Is anyone in there?" I called into the dark forest. My eyes searched for a path into the wood.

"Mmmm," came the voice again.

Toto looked at me and I returned his gaze. "What should we do, Toto?"

Toto gave a sharp bark and began pulling me between the trees and through the brush. Next thing I knew, I was standing in a glade with towering trees all around us, sunlight blinding me. My dog wasn't nearly as blinded. He pulled me to a tall standing tree stump with something shining tethered to it with rope. I put my hand over my eyes. The only thing I hadn't packed were my sunglasses. As my eyes adjusted to the light, I realized what I was looking at. A man-shaped effigy made of metal.

"Mmmm," came the noise, and the metal effigy wriggled against the unforgiving ropes that bound it to the stump.

I stepped closer and saw its eyes move. This wasn't an effigy; it was a man. A tin man. But he wasn't gagged. Instead, his lips were merely closed, and I could see the problem. He had lines of rust along the crease, and along all his joints. Someone had tied him here and left him to rust.

"Mmmm!" he said again.

I glanced at Toto, then back at the tin man, noticing a hatchet and an old oil can sitting on top of the stump behind him. Clearly, this was the work of a sick prankster. Grabbing the hatchet, I cut through the rope, then I took the oil can, full to the brim, and squirted a bit at every joint I could find. It took a few minutes, but finally, the tin man opened his jaw wide and began moving his arms like someone who was stiff from sitting too long.

"What the hell happened to you?" I asked, frowning.

"Did anyone follow you here?" he asked, looking around.

"No."

Then his eyes settled on Toto. "What's that?"

"My dog? His name is Toto." In response, Toto began sniffing at the creature's legs and wagging his tail.

"Oh. We should get out of here. It's not safe," he said. His eyes darted in all directions. From a hollow inside the stump, he reached in and pulled out a leather satchel. Then he collected the hatchet and the oil can, tossed them inside, and threw the bag over his still rusty shoulder. "Come on." He tried to grab my hand, but I pulled it away.

"Who are you?" I asked.

"I'm Jason, the woodsman. Now, come on." He began herding Toto and me out of the clearing and back into the forest.

This was a detour I hadn't anticipated, but to be clear, I wasn't afraid because I had witch powers, and Toto, my loyal familiar, would attack on my command. We walked a few minutes into the dark wood before the tin woodsman, Jason, stopped and took a deep, relieved breath.

"So, you want to tell me what happened?" I leaned back on the nearest tree to take some weight off my weary feet. I was going to need a pedicure after this.

"Five days ago, I was attacked from behind, lost consciousness, and when I woke up, I discovered my attacker had tied me to that tree stump." He took another deep, drawn breath and looked at me. "What are you doing in these woods? I've never seen you here before."

"I was magically transported here during a tornado, and I'm going to see a wizard to find out how to get back. Oh, and my house fell on a witch named Gertrude and crushed her to death." I let out a sigh. It sounded ridiculous when I said it aloud.

"The Wizard, that bastard," Jason said wryly. "He's worthless, if you ask me. The crime in these woods has gotten out of hand. People cutting down trees, tying up woodsmen!"

I winced. "Is there no police presence in Oz?"

Jason rolled his eyes. "The Emerald Palace has guards to protect the Wizard, but..."

"Well, maybe you should come with me to speak to him, and I can find my way home and you can talk to him about the crime in the woods." I only suggested it because I thought it would be nice to have someone to talk to for the long walk. If we lost daylight and had to camp, at least I'd have someone I could use for protection other than Toto.

"Do you think it would help?" He looked at me as if he'd never even considered the idea of taking his governance complaints to the people in charge.

This really was a strange place. I shrugged. "It couldn't hurt. The people in charge need to know what the citizens want and need. You can't just sit idly by and complain. It's always best to change things through action."

He nodded, then gave me a consternated look. "Wait, did you say you killed Gertrude?"

"Yes. I mean, not on purpose. It was an accident. My house landed on her." I winced. "It was an unfortunate event."

"Yeah, well, she was an unpleasant woman. That's probably some of the best news I've had in months." Then he looked at me and Toto. "It's going to be dark soon. We should find a safe place to camp for the night and continue to the Emerald City tomorrow."

I wasn't sure how to respond. "Okay."

We started walking again. All the while, I was curious about Gertrude. Literally, no one liked the woman, and I had to find out why. Maybe it was because I secretly loved a good drama, or maybe it was because I wanted to figure out just how pissed Janice would be when she learned about her sister's demise. Toto and I followed Jason through the woods until we reached a much smaller clearing than the one we'd found him in.

"This is a good spot," he said, dropping his leather satchel to the ground and pulling out his hatchet. "I'll chop some wood for the fire. Could you get together some kindling?"

I nodded and took off my pack, then began scouring the ground for small twigs, with Toto by my side helping the best he could. Once I'd found the twigs and some rocks to encircle the fire, and once Jason had gotten us some firewood, Toto and I settled down with my pack between us. We watched as Jason expertly set the kindling aglow, and before long, the wood flickered to life with orange-gold flames licking skyward.

The silence of the forest and the crackling of the fire soothed me somehow. Toto snuggled next to me and put his head in my lap. "So, what was Gertrude's story? Why did everyone hate her so much?"

Jason looked over at me, then motioned to himself. "Do you see this? She did this to me. I was once a man. A normal man. She cast nasty magic, turning men into creatures and creatures into men." He shook his head. "I'm not the only person she experimented on."

Awkward, I thought. "Oh, wow. Sorry to hear that."

"I thought maybe once she was dead, the spell would die with her, but that's not the case." There was a hint of sadness in Jason's voice. "I was just minding my business in the woods. That's my job, you see. Woodsman. I fell dead trees, plant others, keep the trails trimmed."

I nodded. "Like a forest ranger."

He gave me a strange look.

"That's what we call them where I come from," I explained with a smile.

"So, what is it you do…" His brow furrowed. "What's your name? I don't recall if you told me or not."

"Dorothy, from Kansas," I said.

"Dorothy from Kansas, what is it you do?"

I thought for a moment. How could I explain my online business without it sounding like I was anything like Gertrude? Because I was pretty sure Jason wasn't too keen on witches. "I make bath and body products for people," I said, hoping that didn't elicit any adverse reactions.

"Ah. You run an apothecary." He nodded as if in understanding.

"Yes. Exactly." Then I breathed a sigh of relief because, in this world, no one viewed an apothecary as witchcraft. Whereas in some parts of Kansas, even yoga instructors were witches to some people.

I noticed then that it wasn't particularly cold, though the heat from the fire felt good against my skin. Petting Toto's head, I leaned into him and wondered if Mark had noticed that we were missing. Maybe, but maybe not. I closed my eyes and focused on the sound of my breathing. That night I dreamt of pale-faced witches flying on broomsticks against the backdrop of a full moon, cackling as they went.

The Straw Man

I opened my eyes a slit, staring up at the stars above, the long branches of the trees reaching toward the still-dark sky. Toto was no longer next to me, and I was cold. Sitting up, I saw Jason's metal silhouette standing a few yards away, looking into the sky. "Toto?" I looked around, finally finding him standing a few feet from Jason and looking up, too. "What is it?" I asked.

"We need to put out the last few embers and get moving. It's not safe here. Janice and her army of winged horrors are on patrol. We should stick to the underbrush." Jason came over to the fire and began throwing dirt onto it. There were only a few embers left.

I sat up and brushed the leaves and dirt from my hair, realizing I hadn't brought a hairbrush. That didn't matter right now. If I looked like a disheveled homeless woman by the time I reached the Emerald City, surely the Wizard would understand. And if he didn't, well... my thoughts were cut short when Toto let out a low growl.

My blood ran cold. Springing to my feet, I grabbed my pack, slung it over my shoulder, and took up Toto's leash. Together, we followed Jason back into the forest. I paused and looked back to see two short, shaggy, lumbering figures slowly moving toward our now vacant campsite.

Jason put a finger to his silvery lips and in my mind, I instructed Toto to remain quiet. The dog listened, but began pulling at his leash, away from the campsite and whatever creatures were now investigating it. With my heart pounding in my chest, I followed Toto and Jason, not knowing which direction we were heading and not caring. As long as we were far away from whatever those things were—that's what mattered.

We paused fifteen minutes later, in silence, to listen. I swore I heard someone or something cackle high above the tree line.

"Was that Janice?" I asked, remembering my dream.

Jason nodded wordlessly.

So it wasn't a dream, I thought, and that made me shiver even more. We started moving again. The movement warmed me and soon, a soft light grew in the sky as dawn approached. My stomach growled. The day before had been so eventful, I'd forgotten to eat, and Toto must have been starving.

"Can we stop for some breakfast?" I asked Jason, who stood next to me, unmoving.

He turned toward me. "We'd have to catch something. I don't have provisions."

Slinging my pack from my shoulder, I produced two granola bars and a baggy of dog food for Toto, along with his water bowl. We ate quietly, scanning our surroundings for any signs of life, but there was nothing. Not even birds or squirrels.

"Where is all the wildlife?"

Jason shoved the last bit of the granola bar into his mouth and chewed slowly, then held up the wrapper as if he wasn't sure what to do with it.

I took it from him and shoved the trash into my pack. "You have to have birds or small mammals somewhere in Oz."

"We used to," he said. "You can still trap rabbits, but even those are growing scarce. Sometimes you'll happen upon a lion."

Gulping, I looked at him in disbelief. "Lions?"

He nodded. "Yes."

"What do they live on if there are no small animals anywhere?" I pulled Toto close and rubbed the top of his head, then picked up his empty water bowl. For the first time, I feared for our safety.

"Rodents mostly. They're here, likely just hiding."

I had to ask, even though I wasn't sure I wanted the answer. "Where did all the animals go?"

"Gertrude used hundreds, if not thousands, of them in her experiments." He looked away nervously. "She made them into abominations now controlled by her sister, Janice."

Damn, I thought. Janice really was a wicked witch, and the fact that the Wizard and his guards did nothing about it was pissing me off. Who was this guy anyway? And why wasn't he taking care of his people? Oz would be better off with a stronger leader, and in that moment, I fully intended to tell him so when I met him face to face. "Let's go. We need to get back to the road and make sure we're still heading in the right direction."

"This way," Jason said. "It's probably safe now."

Probably. The word lingered in the air between us for a moment. For all I knew, Jason had bad intentions, too. I mean, who tied up an innocent stranger and left them for dead in the forest? But I didn't get a bad feeling from him, and he hadn't tried to hurt me or Toto. While I was still on high alert, I had to have faith that he knew where we were and that he wanted to see the Wizard as much as I did. I had so many questions about this place, but my need to see the yellow road and a hint of civilization took precedence.

It took a while, but we finally made it back to the road. Again, in the distance, I could see the spire from the city closer now, and still jutting into the sky like a beacon. But now, I could see how its surface glinted in the morning sunlight like a jewel. *Emerald*, my mind corrected.

Ahead of us, the trees receded to reveal farmland. Fields of grain took over the landscape, and one could tell a significant part of the forest had been cleared for this. "Just like home," I said.

"You come from those who work the land?" Jason asked.

It was a weird way to phrase the question, but I nodded. "I come from five or more generations of Kansans on both sides." Witchy land-working Kansans, but Kansans, nonetheless.

We kept along the road when suddenly, a rock went whizzing by my head and a crow, or its Oz equivalent, flew violently away from a field.

"You little bastard! Get outa here, I tell ya!" A strange man emerged from the tall grain, fist raised with a slingshot in the other hand.

I took a few more steps forward just to make sure I was actually seeing things clearly. The man looked like a scarecrow. A straw-filled scarecrow.

"What are you looking at?" he asked.

I glanced at Jason, then turned back to him. "Sorry, I've never seen a..."

"A talking scarecrow," Jason finished for me. "Dorothy, this is Gary. Gary, Dorothy, from Kansas." Then he paused and looked down at my German shepherd. "And this is her dog, Toto."

The scarecrow, Gary, marched right up to us on the side of the road and looked at Toto. "Hide that from Gertrude. She'll turn it into another one of Janice's ferocious beasts."

"About that," I said with another cringe. "Gertrude is dead."

The scarecrow, with his weird straw body but human eyes and lips, stepped back, almost in disbelief. "Dead? No shit."

A lopsided smile slid onto the tin-man's face. "It's true. Janice sent her flying monkeys to raid our camp earlier. I think word of her sister's demise has finally reached her."

Both men looked at me as if expecting me to answer for my actions. "Well, she can't be mad at me for it. It was an accident," I said. Then, I changed the subject. "Was that a crow I just saw?"

Gary nodded. "Damn things keep eating the grain. Why?"

"I think that's one of the few non-humanoid creatures I've seen here so far." I shrugged, then pointed to the slingshot in his hand. "Does that work?"

With a snort, Gary looked at the slingshot with disgust. "It's useless. I applied for a musket license over a year ago and have heard nothing. Unless I have that license, this is my only way to scare them off. The crows have long since stopped finding me scary."

The more I heard about Oz and its problems, the more I felt angry for the people. There were no police, and they suffered from high crime and environmental destruction. And now, the people had been left in the lurch without proper means to defend themselves and the fruits of their labor. It sounded like some of the problems we faced back home—though here it felt more devastating.

"Well, Jason and I are heading to the Emerald City—me to find out how to get back home, and Jason to talk to the Wizard about crime and more police presence. Maybe you should come with us to figure out what happened with your musket license." It seemed a logical suggestion.

Gary considered this briefly. "Why not?"

"Exactly," I said. "At worst, they could tell you your application was denied, but at best, you'll come home with a license."

"Let me grab a few things." Gary disappeared back into the tall shafts of grain, leaving Jason, Toto, and me, waiting. In the distance, I heard the familiar sound of a small engine coming toward us from the direction in which we'd come.

Jason took me by the elbow to pull me off the road, and I pulled Toto's leash, just in time to avoid the motorcycle and the person in all white riding it. The rider raised a white-gloved hand as they passed and kept going, not even slowing down.

"Who was that? I saw them yesterday after my house landed."

Jason shrugged. "Someone from the Emerald City would be my guess."

I frowned—my eyes drifting over the beautiful landscape of Oz. Everything was so green here, but in the distance, it almost appeared as though the landscape turned gray. I pointed to it. "What happened there?"

"It's nothing to be concerned about," he said rather quickly, his eyes traveling back to the field of tall grain as if impatiently waiting for the scarecrow, Gary.

Now, I may not be a college-educated witch, but I know for a fact when someone tells you not to be concerned about something, you should probably be concerned. Very concerned. "I'm not concerned, just curious," I prodded.

He let out a heavy sigh. "Many years ago, a wizard named Oz ruled the land. Apparently, he was rather evil. It was the good Wizard and Glenda who drove him out, but not before the northern half of Oz was destroyed by a plague of darkness. What you see there," he pointed back to the stark gray against the foreground of green, "is where the decimation stopped."

"Oh. Who's Glenda?"

"The Good Witch of the South."

My brow furrowed. "That suggests there are good witches of all the directions."

"Well, there was a Good Witch of the North, but," Jason motioned to the gray in the distance.

"Oh, I see," I said, understanding. "And what about east and west?"

"Those are the bad witches. Janice is the Wicked Witch of the West. Gertrude was the Wicked Witch of the East," he explained, his face void of emotion.

"Well, at least now you only have one wicked witch left," I said.

"Mmm," he said in acknowledgment.

Finally, the grain parted, and Gary emerged with a pack. "I had to get the copies of my paperwork and some food," he said. "And make sure I put up the temporary scarecrow in my stead."

"Did Gertrude…" I motioned to him, hoping it wasn't rude, but I had to know, even though I was pretty sure I already knew the answer.

He nodded. "Damn woman was mad because I kept slingshotting her crows. Told me I'd serve Oz better as a scarecrow. One breath of magic dust, and I fell asleep. I woke up like this."

"But you still chased off her crows," I said, wondering why Gertrude hadn't just killed him.

Gary shook his head. He appeared to know what I was thinking because he'd probably wondered the same thing. "Yes, but I think she found it amusing to leave me like this rather than kill me outright."

Jason clapped his metal hands together. "Well, let's go. If we start now, we can be in the Emerald City by morning."

The three of us, and Toto, began walking again. We stopped for lunch and to fill our water bottles. Lunch was courtesy of Gary who'd brought a loaf of bread, jerked meat, and big hunks of cheese. There was plenty to share. As the late afternoon sun started waning, the landscape changed from farmland to more mountainous terrain. Outcroppings of rock towered above us on either side of the road.

"Let's camp off the road, in those rocks up there," Jason said. "There might be a cave."

My eyes traveled to the area he pointed at. He was probably right. So, we moved up the steady incline, through a mess of large rocks, and into a clearing. There was a cave there, but it looked tight—only big enough to fit one person through at a time, and it was anyone's guess how big it was inside.

"Let's just camp here," I said. "That cave is small, and likely full of bats."

"And mice," Gary said with a shudder. Then looked at me, saying, "They're always trying to steal my straw for bedding, or sleep inside me. It's unsettling."

I nodded in understanding.

Jason, however, wasn't keen on camping in the clearing. "If Janice sends her scouts out, they'll easily see us from the sky. I'll go into the cave and check it out, and if it's big enough and safe, then we'll go in one by one. It will be safer in there than out here."

He had a point. Though I was with Gary. I had no desire to sleep in a dark cave. At the same time, I didn't want to come face to face with the hairy flying creatures—monkeys Jason had called them—in the middle of the night.

Of Lions and Lynxes

Just as Jason's feet disappeared into the cave, there was a deep, resounding growl from inside. I'd never seen anyone back out of a hole that fast. He would have been able to get to his feet quickly had he not been made of metal. Instead, he fell onto his back and dragged himself backward as a large cat, the size of a lynx, crept out of the cave, fangs bared and claws out. Toto, however, was larger than the lynx and bolted forward. Had I not been holding the leash, he might have overtaken the other animal and scared it off. He was approximately forty pounds heavier and larger than the small wild cat.

"Toto!" I yelled. "Sit." Begrudgingly, Toto sat next to me and continued to growl.

"Ugh, lion!" Gary yelled, jumping behind me.

The lynx hissed.

"That's a lynx," I told him. "Not a lion."

"I don't care what it is, get it away from me," Jason yelled, still trying to get to his feet.

The lynx stopped hissing and sat back on its haunches. "What are you doing here?" it asked.

Even Toto stopped growling and tipped his head in confusion. It wasn't every day a wild cat spoke up for itself.

"Camping. Trying to stay out of sight of the Wicked Witch's minions," I said. I could feel straw hands on my back as Gary peeked over my shoulder.

"You're not spelunkers?" the lynx asked.

"What?" Jason and I asked simultaneously.

"Cave explorers," the cat clarified.

"Gods no," I said. With that, I handed Toto's leash to Gary and walked over to help Jason back to his feet. It was a chore because he weighed a ton.

Then I turned to the lynx. "Let me guess, you're another one of Gertrude's creations?"

The cat snorted. "Of course."

"Well, I'm Dorothy. This is Jason, that's Gary, and that's my dog, Toto," I said, introducing us.

In any other scenario, I might have thought I was dreaming, or that I'd accidentally ingested something hallucinogenic. Yet, the fact that I felt fine minus some aches and pains from walking and sleeping on the ground, and that I could pinch myself and feel it, told me that all of this was very real. Bizarre and nightmarish, but painfully authentic.

The cat put one paw to his chest. "I am Liam the lion." The way he said it smacked of pride.

"It's nice to meet you, Liam. Any ideas on how we can avoid flying monkeys tonight?"

Both Jason and Gary gave me a shared, strange look.

"What? He would know. He lives in these mountains." I shrugged. I didn't see what was so weird. I mean, Jason was a tin woodsman, Gary was a living, breathing scarecrow, and Liam was a talking lynx who identified as a lion. Who was I to judge? In all of Oz, the only ones out of place were me and Toto. We must have seemed like strange creatures to all of them.

Liam narrowed his eyes. "Fine, come in, but only for one night," he said.

"Deal," I agreed.

One by one, we followed Liam into the cave beyond. Toto went ahead of me, eager to get closer to Liam, and I squeezed in last, feeling my hips snag slightly as I dragged my body through the tight space. My claustrophobia subsided once we were inside because the cave opened up into a large space. Somewhere deeper into the cave, I could hear water trickling. Light poured in through a few small holes in the mountainside above us.

"We need a fire," Jason said.

"We don't need a fire. It should stay warm enough. What we need is light," I said, pulling a flashlight from my pack. I set it upright and turned it on, the bright beam of light spreading up to the ceiling. There were no bats, probably because it wasn't safe living in a cave with a predator. The only thing we had to worry about was how long the light would last before the batteries gave out.

"Where are you traveling to?" Liam asked after a brief bout of uncomfortable silence.

"The Emerald City," I said. "Toto and I need to find a way home. Jason needs to talk to the Wizard about more security and combating high crime rates in the woods, and Gary needs to find out what's going on with his musket license."

Liam gave Gary a wary look. "What do you need a musket for?"

Gary appeared offended. "To shoot at crows and scare them off, so they don't destroy the grain."

"As long as you don't plan to go lion hunting," Liam said.

"No, why would I do that?"

"Food is scarce, and hunting is a thing of the past in Oz," he said. "It's bad enough people keep invading my house just to explore." I could swear the cat was frowning.

"Maybe you need to talk to the Wizard about property rights and nature conservation," I suggested. "You can come with us if you want."

Liam sneezed and shook his furry head. "I can't imagine the Wizard would listen to a lion."

"I'll make him listen to you," I said firmly. "I can't see why he'd deny any of Oz's citizens an audience. Except maybe Janice."

A chorus of all but me and Toto muttered, "Janice," with disdain. I wondered then if Janice knew how much people hated her, and if that is what reinforced her wicked ways. Then again, some people, psychopaths anyway, enjoyed inflicting pain on others and didn't care what they thought.

"Dorothy?" Jason asked, pulling me from my thoughts.

"Yes?"

"What if the wizard doesn't care about our problems?" A deep frown had settled onto Jason's lips. *If he wasn't careful, he really would freeze that way,* I thought, noting how a few days out in the elements had caused him to rust.

"Well, he cared enough to get rid of the guy who caused the plague on the northern part of Oz, so he has to care what is happening to the people, right? He probably just doesn't know because he's a city guy. I doubt he gets out into the country much," I said with a shrug. My response seemed to satiate my new friends. We ate dinner, more of Gary's bread and cheese, deciding to keep the jerked meat for the following day, and talked about solutions for the residents of Oz and their rural community until late into the night. Finally, I curled up with Toto under the blanket I carried in my bag, and we slept.

"Oh, there's someone in here," came a voice from the mouth of the cave.

I jumped up and Toto let out a bark. My new friends also shook themselves awake. A few hazy beams of sunlight from openings in the rock above made it easier to see around the cave in the day.

"Let me see," said another male voice.

A moment later, a man came squirming through the mouth of the cave.

"Excuse me," I said as he pulled his head through, looking up at me, surprised. "This is someone's home."

"Oh." He didn't bother looking around, just shimmied back out of the opening.

I followed and emerged into the bright morning sun to find three startled men standing there, all about the same height with red hair and gray clothing. They had with them ropes and other supplies fit for rock climbing.

Covered in dust from head to toe, crazy unkempt hair, and no coffee, I must have looked a mess. Toto scurried out behind me, teeth bared, growling. "Relax, Toto," I told him, then I pointed to the cave. "My friend, Liam, lives here."

"There weren't any posted signs," the one standing between the others said.

"Well, we'll soon rectify that," I said with a frown. "You can't just go into unmarked caves when you don't know if someone is living in them."

"We do it all the time," the one to the left said. "Sometimes you see an animal, but..." He shrugged, then looked at me strangely as if noticing my attire for the first time. "Why are you dressed so oddly?"

"Because I stayed the night in my friend's cave on the way to the Emerald City," I said.

Behind me, my friends, one by one, emerged from the cave. Jason last with my pack and blanket in tow, along with his own satchel.

The three men stood there, their eyes growing wider as each of my friends stood up and stepped beside Toto and me. Liam sat next to Toto and licked a paw.

Finally, the guy in the middle glanced at his friends. "Let's go. Tainted by witchcraft, all of them. Cave's probably cursed."

Muttering their dissatisfaction, the men moved off in the opposite direction from the Emerald City, further into the mountainous terrain.

"You need to get a private property sign," I told Liam.

Liam looked at me with golden eyes and lifted a paw. "No opposable thumbs, remember?"

"Okay. While we're in the Emerald City, we'll get one and maybe Jason and Gary can put it up for you," I suggested. *Or maybe you could just try to remove the spell or whatever Gertrude did to them*, my conscience observed wryly. "Or maybe we could see about the witch and wizard trying to take the spells off of all of you."

"Glenda tried."

I frowned. I was growing suspicious of both this wizard and the good witch for their sheer lack of caring. Then and there, I could have told my new friends that I was a witch, too, and that I'd try to remove the spells on them. But I knew how to read a room. It was probably best to still keep it to myself. "Maybe we'll ask again. If the wizard and Glenda stopped everything from dying, maybe together they can figure it out."

I noticed a glimmer of hope in all their eyes and gave them a broad smile, trying to brighten the mood. "Let's have a light breakfast."

With mumbles of agreement all around, we pooled our resources of jerked meat, two granola bars, and some berries from a bush near Liam's cave, and everyone got fed. Then, we packed up our things and continued on our journey to the Emerald City.

We exited the mountainous terrain just after lunch, and as we crested a hill, for the first time, I could see the walls of the city. Suddenly, it felt like Toto and I might see home again. "Why the wall?"

"To keep Janice's armies out," Liam said.

"But," I turned to Jason, "didn't you say they were *flying* monkeys?"

"Oh, she has other things. Yeti, rhinoceroses. And even a dragon," Jason said, his voice assuring me as if he'd seen these things.

"Still doesn't make sense there's a..." I closed my mouth as I saw a shimmer of green, just for a second, over all of Oz. "Oh. Protection spell," I said. Why hadn't I thought of that? I shook my head. "Come on. Let's get this over with."

My friends seemed to harbor the same sentiment. Toto, however, raced along in front of us. For the first time, I saw wildlife. Toto began chasing random squirrels and birds as we went. There were more animals here, close to the Emerald City, probably because they could get some protection from the spell. Down the hill we went, the incline welcome to our tired legs. The city grew closer and closer until we stood ten yards away from the front gate.

"Who's going to knock?" Gary asked, adjusting the straw in his belly that had shifted since lunch.

Everyone's eyes turned to me, including Toto's. "We have to knock?" That seemed weird, but then, compared to everything I'd already witnessed, one more abnormality would not surprise me.

I marched to the small door next to the large, closed gate and knocked roughly. Thirty seconds went by, and I knocked again.

From beyond the door, I heard someone grousing. "I'm coming," came the sour voice from the other side. Then, instead of opening the actual door, he opened the wicket gate in the top of the door. "What do ya want?"

Wow, rude, I thought. What I said, however, was, "Hi, we're here to see the Wizard."

The man's eyes drifted past me to my friends, then back to me. "You can't come in."

"Can I ask why?"

"No," he said, and shut the little wooden window in my face.

My insides quivered with anger, but I kept my calm and knocked again. Harder this time.

The little window slid open. "I told you to go away."

I lowered my voice so that my new friends didn't hear the conversation between the guard and me. "If you don't go tell the Wizard I'm here—and if he doesn't see me—I'm going to take down this nice little protection spell you have here and invite Janice over for tea."

The little man's eyes grew wide with fear. "Wait here," he growled, then forcefully slid his little window shut before huffing off.

I'd never threatened anyone with witchcraft before, not seriously anyway. Sure, I'd gotten caught up in a few petty online witch wars in my younger years, but it was all shit-talk, no action. This time, however, if they didn't comply, I'd have to follow through, and I wasn't so sure I could do it.

What I'd said worked though, because the wicket door stayed closed, and eventually the main door was opened. The same angry old man let me, my dog, and my friends into the Emerald City.

Power Couple

"Follow me," a guard dressed in a crisp green uniform told us.

We left the cranky old man behind us and followed the guard down the yellow cobblestone road toward the highest tower. As we went, green- and orange-haired residents paused from their daily lives to watch as two cursed men, a lynx, and a young woman and her dog were led through the city by one of the Wizard's guards.

I tried to smile at a few people, but when I caught their eyes, they turned their heads quickly, as if looking me in the eye would curse them. By their expressions of awe, I could tell Jason, Gary, or Liam had never set foot inside the city before, which seemed odd. But then how many people lived their whole lives in a single place and rarely, if ever, traveled? Not me, but quite a few, I imagined.

When we came to the palace, another door with yet another wicket gate and another angry old guy opened, and we were led across a courtyard into a large room with marble floors and a golden throne beneath two large glass-stained windows and an emerald roof.

The guard, who'd only said two words to us, instructed, "Wait here." Then he disappeared from the room.

In the distance, I was sure I heard the engine of a motorcycle.

There was a crackle, a bright flash of light and some smoke, and there he was. A man dressed in a pressed gray suit wearing a long black cape and top hat. Just like the trope of an early twentieth-century stage magician. Reflexively, I clapped. His entrance, though showy, had been exciting. "Bravo," I said.

"As I see it, young lady, you're not in a position to be rude or make demands." He frowned at me.

Behind us, the heavy doors swung open and the clickety-clack of boots against marble caused us all to turn. It was the motorcycle rider in white. She pulled off her helmet and white gloves, which both vanished in a flash, and then ran her long, slender fingers through her bleached-blond hair. Whoever the cyclist was, she looked like all the women on *Real Housewives* combined.

"I came as soon as I heard," she called, striding toward our small group with a practiced appraisal of us. "Which one is the witch?"

"This one," the Wizard said, pointing to me.

My new friends, their eyes unable to mask how betrayed they felt, stepped away from me. It was going to happen at some point. I'd just hoped they wouldn't find out at all or that the news wouldn't reach them until I was gone.

"What is it you want from us?" the Wizard asked.

"A few things," I said. "First, I'm Dorothy. Dorothy Gale, from Kansas. And this is my dog, Toto. A tornado and portal brought me here. I need help getting home." I turned to my friends then. "These are my friends who live right here in Oz with you. The woodsman, Jason, who was turned into a tin man by Gertrude. He needs to talk to you about providing a police force in the rural areas. The crime is getting bad. Next, this is Gary. He was turned into a scarecrow by Gertrude. He's just trying to run his farm and feed the people of Oz, and yet he has to use a slingshot to scare the birds and rodents away or risk them eating all of his crops. All because he still hasn't received his musket license. And finally, there's my friend Liam, turned into," I paused because everyone called Liam a lion, even though he was clearly a lynx, "a lion by Gertrude, who has to deal with cave explorers trampling through his house a few times a week because his cave isn't considered protected land or private property under the law."

My eyes went from the Wizard to the super-model woman who was busy admiring her long nails, and back to the Wizard.

The smile on the woman's lips grew slightly, and she reached out her hand. "I'm Glenda, and this is my boyfriend, the Wizard, Herman." She nodded at the Wizard. "We can help you with all your needs, but we need you to do something for us."

"We do?" the Wizard, Herman, asked.

She put a single finger up to Herman's lips. "Trust me." Her eyes narrowed, and she turned to me. "Is it true that you killed Gertrude?"

I was so tired of having to explain it, but didn't have a choice. "Not intentionally. It was an accident. My house landed on her."

"Yes, I saw it land and drove by as you were talking to the people of Munchkin." Glenda went and sat on the throne, and the Wizard hurried to her side like the obedient servant he was.

"And didn't stop," I said, quickly questioning if being sarcastic was the right move.

She waved a hand absently. "Well, I had no idea the house landed on anyone. Besides, one wicked witch dead is happy news for us all. How would you like to earn yourself a fast one-way ticket home?"

I didn't have a good feeling about this. "And what about the police patrols, musket license, and private property signs—along with turning these three, and all the citizens of Oz who were transformed, back to their original selves?"

"She's a haggler, Hermie," Glenda said.

Herman snickered.

"Well, it's all of that, along with the ticket home or no deal."

Glenda looked at Toto, who sat to my left, staring at her. With one command, I could have ordered him to rip out her throat, and he would have. "Very well. But I need you to do two tiny things for us."

"Well, out with it," I said. Patience had never been my strong suit.

"You need to kill Janice, and you need to destroy *Oz*." Glenda's left eyebrow went up on the intonation of *Oz*.

Jason, Gary, and Liam gasped. "What?" I asked. I'm not destroying the beautiful Land of Oz and all the people. Even if some people are weird. Those folks in Munchkin..." I frowned.

"Not the land itself, you ignorant woman," Herman said, shaking his head. "The dark spirit that inhabits it—Oz. The land is *of* Oz. If you can destroy Oz, those of us who live here can finally be free."

"I'm not a hitman," I said, wondering what the hell I'd just walked into. Maybe it would have been best if I'd just gone back to my house and found a spell to take Toto and me home without any help from these two. Perhaps I even had something in there that would turn Jason, Gary, and Liam back into people. Then *they* could deal with their leaders and their politics. "Besides, you obviously already took out this Oz guy since you're both now in charge. Why can't you take out Janice?"

Glenda paused thoughtfully and pursed her lips. "Oz isn't really destroyed yet. Just sleeping. We were able to subdue him with a few spells I drummed up." Then a strange smile slid over her lips. "Great and powerful Oz no more."

I wondered then if maybe Janice wasn't actually evil, but instead, just reacting to these two. Then again, what Gertrude did to my friends was pretty nasty, and it seemed she was doing her magical spells to support her sister. I frowned.

"Look," Glenda said, examining her perfectly manicured nails. "If you help us, we'll help you. If not, I'm sure you could muster up enough magic to send yourself home."

"You didn't answer my question," I prodded. "Why can't you destroy Janice and her spells by yourself?"

Glenda leaned forward. "Okay, full transparency. We can't get close enough. But you—you might be able to. After all, she's bound to be looking for whoever killed her sister. If you get close enough..." She snapped her fingers at Herman and held out her hand. He reached into his cloak and pulled out a beautiful green bottle with a cork in it and set it in Glenda's palm. Glenda held the bottle out to me. "Take this, add it to some water, and douse her with it. Full strength might work, too."

I took the bottle, peering through the translucent green glass to the clear liquid inside. "What is it?"

"Witches, you see, we tend to melt when this touches us." Then she shrugged. "Be careful not to get it on yourself."

"A melting potion?" I asked, holding the bottle further from me.

"Something like that." She pointed at Jason. "He's made of tin. Take him with you. Have him pour it on her. The potion won't hurt him. Might just scuff him a bit."

"It's acid," I said in disbelief. "You want me to throw acid on her?"

Glenda put on an innocent, beaming smile. "She'll melt into a puddle."

She was fucking nuts. "And Oz?"

Glenda pointed to a copper urn on a side table on the left side of the room. "He's in there. Non-corporal. Maybe you have something in your witchy arsenal to vanquish him?"

I doubted it, but said nothing. Instead, I looked at my new friends, who still seemed wary with the new information that I, too, was a witch. How did Glenda know anyway? Did witches here give off some kind of energy that the others could sense?

"I'll do it," Jason said, giving me a curt nod. "Only if you promise to keep your word. Once Janice is dead, you send Dorothy home, free us from Gertrude's spells, and then work with us to clean up the Land of Oz, provide laws for private property, and speed up local licensing."

"I'm in, too," Gary said firmly.

Liam wasn't as quick to jump in, but he finally nodded. "Fine, I'm in, but I hate monkeys."

I couldn't believe what I was hearing. Was I actually going to do this? Act like a terrorist and throw acid on a woman? *She is a wicked witch*, my mind reasoned. *Look what her sister did to Jason, Gary, and Liam.* But what if she wasn't? History was full of women wrongly accused of being wicked. Hell, even *I* had enemies who thought I was evil incarnate. While her sister had taken much of this land's wildlife and transformed it into something grotesque and unnatural, what if Janice *was* the *nice* one? I let out a heavy sigh. "Fine. I'll do it, but I swear, if you break your promises..." I left the sentence hanging there in the air between us, intentionally threatening.

Glenda waved us off like a queen dismissing her servants. "Off you go then."

Inwardly, I seethed. If I were the confrontational type, I likely would have smacked her upside her pretty, smug face. Instead, I turned on my heel. "Come on, Toto," and stomped from the palace with Jason, Gary, and Liam close behind. Once we were outside, no one was there to guide us out of the Emerald City. It was as if we'd been cast out and no one cared if we were here or not. I began walking toward the way we'd come in.

"Dorothy?" Jason called from behind me.

I kept walking.

He caught up to me and grabbed my elbow. "Wait, you're mad, I know."

Whirling around, our eyes met, and he recoiled slightly. I was a witch, after all. "Those two," I started, pointing back at the palace, castle, whatever, "they're no better than the witches. Or Oz." I shook my head. "Didn't you tell me Oz was dead? Why didn't you tell me they were keeping him in an urn—asleep?"

"I didn't know. Also, I didn't think Oz mattered anymore. I thought Glenda and the Wizard had stopped him. Destroyed him." He shrugged, then glanced back at our other companions.

"Maybe, as we go, you can start at the beginning and tell me the entire story so that I fully know what I'm getting into." I began walking again, Toto tugging at the leash ahead of me as if he were anxious to get out of the Emerald City.

We camped about a mile outside the city that night. Over a crackling fire, Jason started the story. "When I was a child, Oz ruled this land. Things were fine, and people were happy."

"So, Oz wasn't evil?" I hated to interrupt.

"No. Not that I recall. We didn't have wicked witches and good witches back then either. Just witches, and you'd go to them if you needed an herbal remedy for an illness, things like that." He didn't wait to see if I had more questions, just continued on with the story. "Then, Herman, who was the wealthiest man in the Land of Oz, began building his Emerald City, probably for Glenda, who was a young woman back then. They've always been smitten with one another."

I rolled my eyes but didn't say anything.

"It was after the city was finished that something changed. You see, Oz was an actual man back then. A kind and fair man, and the Land of Oz flourished. I was probably a teenager when things changed. There were rumors that Oz and Herman were fighting, and then rumors that Herman, through magic, had separated Oz from his body. His body died, of course, and it left Oz in a state of limbo. A disembodied spirit cursed to roam the world without a body." He paused to throw another log on the fire. "All of this according to the stories I heard, you understand."

I was glad he paused because I'd gotten a cold chill. "Oz went to the north, to the forests up there, and people said that if you listened to the wind at night, you could hear Oz crying for his lost body. Herman and Glenda, of course, took over immediately, ruling from their Emerald City." Jason stopped, as if not knowing how to continue the story.

"Disembodied spirits eventually lose their humanity and become twisted and malevolent," I said, remembering the few necromancy texts I'd read.

Jason nodded. "Exactly. Oz the spirit was no longer Oz the man, and all he could remember was that the Land of Oz was his, and it was stolen from him by the man who removed him."

"Why wasn't Herman tried for murder?" I asked.

"He told the people that Oz was going to tax them more and impose more rules and that Herman was fighting him on it, and that Oz's death was an accident. They'd allegedly gone up to the mine and Oz slipped, falling into a ravine. The people believed him. The witches did not. Well, except for Glenda. People love Glenda." Jason gave me a half-smile, then frowned. "How come you didn't tell us you were a witch?"

I shrugged. "I didn't think it was relevant, and when it finally was, I was worried you'd be afraid that I was wicked like Janice and Gertrude."

"They weren't always wicked," Jason said. There was a hint of sadness in his voice.

Liam snuggled into Toto's sleeping form and closed his eyes, while Gary sat by wordlessly and just listened to our conversation.

"What were they like before?"

"Gertrude was the more outgoing one. She's the one who vowed to destroy Herman and Glenda and their Emerald City. Janice, my beautiful Janice, she was with her sister. I loved her once." Tears began forming in the corners of his eyes.

I was seeing things a lot clearer now. Herman, likely not a real wizard, had killed Oz in order to take over. Only the witches knew the truth about what happened. When the people had gone along with Herman and Glenda, it had turned the witches against the people as well as the new leader. Oz, likely a real wizard in his disembodied state, had turned malevolent and tried to destroy the land in hopes of getting revenge on the man who killed him.

Then it dawned on me that emeralds were used in protection spells to thwart magic and keep things contained, like angry spirits. And I, Dorothy Gale, had the bad luck to land right in the middle of a war between two witches. One who likely wanted revenge for her sister's death, and the other wanting to use me as a pawn in that war. I had two choices. The first choice—I could do Glenda's bidding and leave Oz in the hands of a murderous couple who had probably planned Oz's demise together. Or, second, I could go straight back to my house and muster up all the magic I could to take Toto and me home, and hope that Janice didn't get to me first.

Wicked Witches

Janice didn't send her flying monkeys. She sent a note instead. We were sitting there, minding our own business, when the note magically manifested on top of my pack in a flash of green smoke. I reached out and picked it up, holding it in my trembling hand.

"Well, what does it say?" Gary asked, wide-eyed and clearly afraid.

I opened it and read it aloud. "*I know you had no control over the death of my sister and that it was an accident. I also saw you went to see the impostor 'wizard' and his trophy witch. Let's meet in the woods near Munchkin tomorrow night, alone, so I can tell you what you need to know. Then you can decide whose side you're on. Cordially, Janice, High Sorceress of the Shadowlands.*"

I folded the note back up.

"Alone," Jason echoed, his eyes staring blankly into the forest. "Will you go?"

"I think I should." I narrowed my eyes at Jason. "Do you really want to throw acid on a woman you used to love?"

His attention came back from wherever it had been. "No."

"You realize that Herman and Glenda are pretty evil, right?" My comment was met with blank stares. "I'm going. Maybe Janice has something important to say."

"While you're there, ask her why she had her sister turn us into," Gary held out his straw arms. "...this."

The accusatory tone immediately put me on the defensive. "I'm not saying Janice is any better. I'm just saying that maybe she felt betrayed by all of you for choosing the wrong side." I shrugged. "Not that any of you deserved such cruelty. I've found that often, behind every evil deed is someone who was hurt or betrayed and, as a result, lost their faith in others."

"Will you choose a side?" Jason asked.

"All I want is to see all of you returned to your former selves and for Toto and me to get back home," I said.

I didn't want to choose a side at all. I just wanted to get the hell out of Oz.

We made it to the forest just outside of Munchkin, close to where I'd initially met Jason, about an hour before sundown.

"Be careful not to touch her," Liam warned, his tail curled around Toto's front legs. "I've heard if you're a witch and you touch a witch, your skin will turn green, and you'll become a wicked witch." It was the first bit of input the lynx had given since we'd left the Emerald City. He and Toto had become close, which didn't surprise me. Toto had always had a soft spot for cats.

"I doubt that's true, Liam. Wickedness is in the heart of the person, and I have no ill will toward anyone," I lied. I did have ill will—toward the impostor wizard and his trophy witch. I smiled. Janice had put it so perfectly, and that alone made me feel as if she were a kindred spirit.

"Well," I said, gathering my courage to go into the forest. "Come on, Toto."

Toto stood, but Liam stepped into his path. "You're supposed to go alone. What if she tries to harm Toto?"

I had mixed feelings about this. My black German shepherd was my constant companion, and I couldn't even imagine leaving him alone with Jason, Gary, and Liam. Maybe Liam was right. If it was a trap, at least I knew Toto would be safe. "Toto, you stay here with Liam and the guys. Keep them safe," I said, my heart sinking into my stomach. "Wish me luck."

They didn't, instead I suspected their worried looks followed me as I disappeared into the forest. Janice hadn't given clear instructions about the exact location of our meeting, and the light was fading fast. I took my flashlight from my backpack. Soon, the night sky loomed above me beyond the canopy of trees. Twigs and dry leaves crunched under my feet, snapping and cracking in the silence. I turned on the flashlight, its beam piercing through the darkness. It felt like a solitary lifeline in the dark and eerie forest. Maybe it was eerie because I didn't know what to expect. Would Janice jump out at me? Not show up? The glow from my flashlight cast dancing shadows on the trees. Above me, the twisted and gnarled branches moved with the wind, the leaves rustling together like an audience gathering to watch my demise. An owl's mournful hoot echoed somewhere far off. I stopped, realizing I'd been holding my breath. I drew in a deep breath, smelling the scent of damp earth and musty, decaying foliage. But the air was crisp and fresh, and after a few more inhales, I felt a little better. Every step forward felt heavier, each breath louder, as I ventured deeper into the forest.

There was a light in the distance. I could see it. A small campfire. I started toward it, and as I got closer, I saw a figure sitting on a log by themselves, occasionally holding their hands up as if to warm them. Drawing closer, I turned off the flashlight and moved slowly, ducking behind trees. Sitting there was a slender woman with long, dark hair. She couldn't have been over fifty. She wore a black dress and black boots. A black shawl covered her shoulders. It was the outfit of someone in mourning.

"Hello?" I called out.

The woman stood.

I stepped out from behind a tree and made my way into the perimeter of light cast by the fire. "Janice?

"I am Janice. You must be Dorothy." She stepped up to me and held out her hand, a look of expectation on her face. Now that I could see her clearly, I noticed a few wisps of gray hair at her temples, and her face was just showing a few fine lines around her mouth and in the corners of her eyes.

Shaking her hand, I nodded.

She turned back toward the fire. "Come. Sit by the fire. It's chilly out here. I would have invited you to my cottage for tea, but I think you understand my caution."

In the woods around us, I heard movement, and I stopped in my tracks.

"I'm surprised you didn't bring your familiar," she said. Clearly, she'd done a divination, because she knew an awful lot about me. On the other hand, I only knew what others had told me about her because I hadn't even considered doing a divination regarding her. Rookie witch mistake, I know, but in my defense, I was new to this witch-war business.

"I left him with the lynx," I said.

"Mm." She sat and patted the fallen log next to her.

"I'm really, really sorry about your sister. I had no idea my house was in the air, let alone heading toward a portal. I was in the bathtub with Toto just trying to ride the tornado out." It all came bubbling out of me before I could stop myself.

The witch looked down at her hands for a moment, and I thought I saw tears in the corners of her eyes. "Thank you. Losing Gertrude was tough, but I knew at some point there would only be one of us left. I'd kind of hoped it would be me who went first."

Not sure what to say, I finally sat down next to her.

After collecting herself for a moment, she put a smile onto her pale lips. "What has happened has happened and I would never consider necromancy." Then she clapped her hands together. "I see you met the Wizard and our resident Good Witch." There was sarcasm in her voice.

I nodded and looked her straight in the eyes. "Yes. They're horrible people."

"You do have good judgment." She sighed. "I'm all alone in fighting them. They have the people under their spell, and my sister is now gone. Maybe I should stop fighting." I'd never heard so much defeat in someone's voice.

"Well, can you blame the people for being on their side? Your sister turned animals into monstrosities and men into dark visages of their former selves."

"Any men who were turned into something unnatural deserved it." She sat up straighter and lifted her chin.

"What did Liam do?"

Janice snorted. "He was working up in that mine of Herman's when Oz had his accident. But he was too cowardly to say or do anything. He saw it all." She lifted an eyebrow. "So Gertrude saw fit to turn him into a cat."

"A lynx that thinks it's a lion," I corrected.

She chuckled. "Well, yes."

"Cats are courageous," I said. "And curious."

Janice shrugged.

"And Gary? Why is he made of straw again?"

"Ah, well, aside from continually shooting my pet crows with that slingshot, that man cares for nothing and no one but his grain. Whenever faced with a serious issue or argument, instead of facing it, he created his own distorted version of it and argued against that. A straw man or scarecrow that could be easily knocked down, seemed fitting. Though I imagine the symbolism was lost on a brainless jerk like him." She flashed me another kind smile. "And let me guess, you're going to ask about Jason next?" This time, I sensed emotion in her voice. There was definitely a story there.

"Yes."

"Well, we used to date as teenagers."

"I figured," I said.

"When I asked him to join me and Gertrude against Herman and Glenda, and told him what happened to Oz, he downright told me to let it go and that it was none of our business. The man has *no heart.* So Gertrude helped me turn him into the tin man he was." This time, she crossed her arms over her chest, and I could almost feel the hurt that radiated from her.

"Was it your..." I paused, searching for the right word. Did I call them familiars? Minions? "...friends who tied him to that tree stump to rust?"

A heavy sigh escaped her lips. "No. Crime has been out of control because Herman and Glenda don't care about the people of Oz. They just care about living their opulent lifestyle while everyone else lives in squalor. My familiars, the monkeys, they are my eyes and ears only. For now. I don't want to put them in harm's way, but I will. I blame Herman and Glenda for everything. Even Gertrude's death. If she hadn't been in that field picking herbs for the potion to keep our protections up—against Glenda—she wouldn't have been there for your house to fall on."

The rustling in the surrounding forest started up again, and I stood.

Janice put out a slender hand. "Don't worry. It's just my familiars."

"Did you turn all of the animals?" I couldn't help asking, especially since Jason had told me how all the animals in the forest were disappearing.

"Oh, no. We simply moved them to a safe place where they could enjoy living and not be hunted. Herman and Glenda can't be trusted to be the stewards of Oz." The witch clapped her hands against her knees. "Well then, are you willing to help me remove Herman and Glenda from power and release Oz's spirit so I can exorcise it to the other side?"

Frozen by the directness of her question, I stood there, speechless. I really disliked Herman and Glenda. My witchy instincts told me that Herman had murdered Oz in cold blood by pushing him into that ravine, and I knew those instincts were never wrong. "It depends."

"Yes?"

"Will you turn Jason, Gary, and Liam back into their former selves and help me get back home?" When she didn't answer immediately, I added, "Because Herman and Glenda thought they could use me to destroy you. You seem to be the only obstacle between them and their absolute power. Well, that and Oz. They have his spirit trapped in an urn in the palace. They seem to think *I* can destroy him once and for all. Those were their demands if any of us wanted their help."

"You saw it?" She narrowed her eyes. "Where they're keeping the spirit of Oz, I mean."

"Yeah."

Janice nodded. "You know why they built the Emerald City then."

"I think so," I said. "To protect themselves from your magic and to keep the spirit of Oz contained. Suggesting they pre-planned Oz's murder."

She stood. "Precisely. Gertrude and I knew something was up when all those emeralds started showing up." Then she took my hands in hers. "Will you help?"

"Will you?" I wasn't giving up my original demands.

"Yes," she said. "I suppose those three have learned their lesson, and you, you have the power to get back home. I'll help you if you need it though."

"Do you know how we're going to do this?" I was hoping she had a plan because I had no idea how this was going to play out, or if any of us would survive it.

"I have a plan. But first, we need to collect my sister's magical shoes." Her brow furrowed.

In my mind's eye, I could still see those silvery red stilettos on the feet under my house. "Her shoes?"

"You're going to need them," she said.

"I don't know if I'd be comfortable wearing a dead woman's shoes," I said.

"Not those ridiculous silver spiked-heel ones she was wearing when she died. No, she enchanted all of her shoes with teleportation abilities. We'll find you another pair," she said matter-of-factly. "They are all made of silver and ruby though. That's part of the magic."

"Oh," I said.

"Come on. Now that I know you're willing to help, I can invite you back to my house. Do you ride a broom?" She didn't bother waiting for my answer. Instead, she clapped her hands and two flying monkeys appeared from the darkness of the surrounding forest, each holding a broom.

Magic Slippers

I ALMOST FELL OFF of the broom—twice. The broom, however, seemed pre-programmed. That programming, I think, helped me stay on somehow. I was so busy hanging on for dear life, that I barely noticed the cool night air rushing against my face and through my hair. When we finally landed, I breathed a sigh of relief. It took me a few minutes to reacclimate to standing on solid ground before I could fully appreciate my surroundings. In the clearing stood a good-sized cottage, encircled by trees. Things were watching us from the dark—I could feel their eyes on us. I followed Janice to the front door, leaning my broom against the wooden siding of the house alongside hers. She opened the door and ushered me in. "Come."

For Oz being such a strange place, Janice's house was quite normal. There was a living room with a small fire in the hearth, a kitchen area with a table and chairs, and a hallway leading to other rooms. Bedrooms or storage, I assumed.

"Have a seat and let me get some shoes for you to try." Janice disappeared into one of the rooms and reappeared with two pairs of shoes, each the same silvery red color as the stilettos on the feet of the woman under my house. The first pair had a small heel. Now, I'm not ashamed to admit that I rarely, if ever, wore heels unless they were chunky. I could never understand how women balanced in heels because I always ended up tripping in them. The second pair, however, were slip-on flats.

I took the flats from Janice. "These might be easier to walk in."

Janice nodded. "I'm not one for the strange shoes either, but my sister liked them." She shrugged. She didn't behave like a woman in mourning, but every time she mentioned Gertrude, there was sadness in her eyes.

Pulling off my boots, I slipped my feet into the strange slippers, feeling them instantly form to fit my size-eight feet. Then I stood and took a few steps in them, like one does when trying on shoes. They were surprisingly comfortable. "These fit incredibly well," I said, surprised.

"Now, to transport yourself, all you have to do is click your heels together three times while visualizing where you want to go, and the shoes will take you there." Janice smiled up at me from the rocking chair she sat on the edge of. "Should you try them?"

I froze. "Where should I go?"

"Let's try something simple. Try going out onto the porch." She gave me a nod as if to say, *okay, do it.*

So I did. I visualized the front porch of Janice's cottage where we'd left the brooms and clicked my heels three times. There was a flash and movement, and I found myself standing outside. The cottage door opened, and Janice had a kind grin on her face. "Well? How was that?"

I felt like I needed to stand there a moment longer to regain my balance because the teleportation threw me off. "Okay. Um, how?"

"The spell involves silver for protection and teleportation, but Gertrude also liked red, so she added chipped rubies. She constructed every pair with a spell for teleportation." She motioned me back into the house. "I'm sure the actual spell is somewhere in the grimoire."

We went back into the living room and sat, the warmth from the fire taking away the faint chill of the air outside.

"Is there a limit to how many times I can use the shoes before the magic wears off?" I pointed my toes, examining the strange, enchanted flats on my feet.

"No. The magic is built into their construction, so they will always be magic." Janice stood. "Tea?"

"Yes, please," I said, noticing for the first time that my mouth was a bit dry. While she made tea, I wondered if I could use the shoes to get home, with Toto in my arms. "If I used the shoes to steal Oz's urn, for example, would I be able to bring it back with me?"

Janice didn't turn from making the tea. "Yes. Anything you hold should come along with you."

"Including a person or an animal?"

She nodded and poured boiling water from a kettle into each cup. "Yes. Are you thinking they might help you get home?"

"They might help," I said, immediately feeling guilty for considering bailing on the Land of Oz in favor of getting myself and Toto home. After all, this witch war between Janice, Glenda, and Herman wasn't my fight. At the same time, my portal-opening potion and my house were part of the reason Janice's sister was dead. Even though it was an accident, I couldn't help but feel bad for her. My house falling on a woman had completely altered the balance of power here. I immediately made sure Janice knew my intention was not to abandon her for my selfish desire to get home. "So what's the plan?"

"To get you home?" she asked, picking up both teacups and bringing them back to the living room. She set them on the small table between us.

"To dethrone the Wizard and Glenda," I corrected. "And send Oz's spirit to the hereafter so it won't harm the people, or Land of Oz, in its revenge-seeking."

She took a sip of her tea, and I followed suit. The hot liquid tasted like fresh herbs with just a touch of honey. It was divine. I greedily took another sip.

Then she set her cup on the table. "We'll have to kill them."

A flood of anxiety rushed through me. "I've never intentionally killed anyone or anything in my life," I said. Then I remembered how Herman and Glenda wanted to send me to kill Janice—with the acid that Jason still had. But it hadn't been me who agreed to that—it had been Jason.

Janice's attention was aimed at her front window then. She beckoned someone or something, and I tensed. The window opened, and two monkeys with wings like bats climbed through the window and closed it behind them. "This is Amy, and this is Sam," she said, introducing the creatures.

The monkeys went to Janice and crawled into her lap, and she gave each one a kiss in the middle of its forehead. "My sweet babies," she said, petting them.

"How... how many do you have?" I'd heard stories about monkeys going berserk and ripping people's faces off, so I didn't want to get any closer than I had to.

"About thirty-five, but these two are my special ones," she said, making cute faces at them like one might to a dog or cat. "How many familiars do you have?"

"Just Toto," I said, feeling guilty that I hadn't brought him with me. I knew Janice wouldn't have minded.

"Oh yes. The strange creature. I've never seen anything like it."

"Dog," I said. "I left him with the guys." A frown covered my lips. What if they harmed him? What if…

Janice stopped my racing thoughts. "They should be here soon."

"What?" No sooner had I asked than a commotion was heard outside.

"Hands off me, you wild creatures!"

I recognized Gary's voice, stood, and ran toward the door. Then there was a bark. Toto. But Toto's bark wasn't one of alarm or fear. Instead, it sounded like he was playing. I threw open the door to see the outlines of my friends. Toto, on the other hand, made sport of chasing one of the winged monkeys, who turned and chased him back. "Toto!" I cried. He whirled around and raced toward me, almost knocking me down when he jumped on me, tail wagging and tongue hanging out of his mouth. "Good dog!"

"Dorothy?" came Jason's voice.

"Jason?" I turned and looked at Janice.

"Well, we need them if the plan is going to work," she said, her voice slightly bitter.

"Janice," Jason greeted, his jaw set. The tension in the air grew thick immediately. It was almost palpable.

"Jason," she said, the distaste clear in her voice. She turned and led us all into the house. We sat around the fire in silence for a few minutes. Janice in one chair with her monkeys, Sam and Amy, me in the other with Toto at my feet, and Jason, Gary and Liam across from us on the floor. The tension grew.

It didn't take me long to lose my patience. "I think maybe you two need to talk. Maybe Liam, Gary and I should go back outside."

"I don't think that's necessary," Jason said.

"Agreed," Janice said. "There's nothing to talk about."

Jason snorted.

Oh, here we go, I thought. I wasn't wrong.

"You made your choice," Janice said coldly.

With all the grace of an anchor, Jason stood, pulled something from his pack and threw it toward me. I caught it. It was the bottle of acid Glenda had given us to pour on Janice.

"You can do it. I'll wait outside," Jason said, turning to leave.

"Hold on a minute," I said. "We're not throwing acid on Janice, but we are going to settle all of your issues with her right now." I had never sounded more like my mother in all my life.

The room went eerily quiet. I set the bottle of acid on the table next to my empty teacup. "Now, here's what we're going to do." I took a calming breath. "Janice, you're going to tell each of them why your sister turned them, and then they will have a chance to respond, and you're all going to talk this out like adults."

"Why would we do that?" Jason asked.

"Because she's your only hope to have you returned to your former state—that's why." I scowled at him.

"But the other witch promised to turn us back if we helped them," Gary said.

"And you believed them?" I closed my eyes and buried my head in my hands for a moment. "I have my doubts about that. Just a feeling."

"And you trust the wicked witch whose sister turned us into beasts—instead of Glenda, who has never harmed any of us?" Jason threw his head back and rolled his eyes.

"Jason, I have a feeling," I started.

"A feeling?"

"Humor me, please? My instincts are never wrong. Besides, if she and her familiars were that evil, Toto would have flipped out," I said, looking down at my dog, who was happily sleeping at my silvery red shoe clad feet.

Janice said nothing, but Jason finally relented. "Very well." His eyes turned to Janice with a hard glare.

All eyes turned to Janice. "Jason, you refused to believe me when I told you what happened to Oz, and when I told you that Herman and Glenda were up to something. You abandoned Gertrude and me to fight this war for the Land of Oz on our own. I thought you loved me. That we were friends. Your heart was so cold, like a man made of steel. This is why my sister did this to you and I didn't stop her."

I could swear I saw Jason wince.

"What do you have to say for yourself?" Janice's icy eyes cut through him as she waited for his response.

"I shouldn't have done that. It probably was an overreaction on my part," he finally conceded. "But it felt like you were overreacting at the time."

"And now?" she asked. "Don't lie either. I will be able to tell if you're just telling me what I want to hear."

"I don't know," Jason admitted. "I don't know what to believe anymore."

That seemed fair enough to me. Jason clearly didn't have the same ability for intuitive discernment as witches did.

"If I turn you back, will you believe that I'm not the one overreacting?" Her voice raised in pitch, but only slightly.

"I would," he said, low and quiet.

Janice stood and waved her hands in a particular shape, intoning words I didn't recognize and slowly, before our eyes, Jason changed. The metal bits of his body softened and seemed to melt away, leaving a man in his fifties with gray hair and a short beard in its wake. Jason paused to look at his hands and touch his face before looking at Janice. "Thank you," he finally said.

Janice simply nodded. I wondered then if their relationship could ever be repaired. I hoped so. Neither of them deserved to be alone for the rest of their lives. Then again, if they hated one another, that was that, and it was none of my business.

"Do me next!" Gary literally took a step toward Janice.

"You are the most impulsive," Janice started.

Not a good start, Janice, I thought.

She continued. "You care for no one but yourself and your grain. You have been cruel to my crows, and you have a one-track mind. You're an idiot. A straw man who buries his head in the sand and sees nothing outside his own wants and desires—even the evil of Herman and Glenda."

Gary looked down at his feet, ashamed.

"What do you have to say for yourself?"

He looked up at Janice. "You're right. I've been very selfish. My life has been my farm. I have turned my war with the crows and the harvest of my grain into my only reasons for living."

"If I turn you back, will you be more considerate of others? If so, I will instruct my crows to stay out of your fields, and I will turn you back into your former self."

"Yes, ma'am," Gary said, and I could tell he meant it.

Another incantation uttered by Janice, and Gary's straw-man façade changed, melting away, leaving a man in his late thirties standing there. He looked up at Janice with a mix of disbelief and joy, as if he never thought he'd see his own flesh again.

"Thank you, ma'am. I won't disappoint you ever again," he said with a quick smile.

"We would all appreciate that. Thank you." Then Janice turned her attention to Liam, who, as usual, had been his timid self. "And you, Liam—you are a coward. We had hoped turning you into a cat would help you grow a spine. You saw Herman murder Oz. You saw it and you did and said nothing." Janice stared him down, waiting for an answer.

Everyone's eyes turned to Liam, who finally nodded. "You're right. I saw everything, but I was afraid Herman would come after me next if he knew I knew. People like that, they won't stop to keep their secrets. I was afraid for my life. I know now I should have told someone, but who?"

I couldn't believe my ears. Liam had actually seen it happen, and yet he'd said nothing to any of us.

"You could have told me," Jason said.

"I didn't know you. I wasn't sure who would turn me in," he said.

Janice let out a sigh. "Well, that's fair. Perhaps my sister and I judged you too harshly." Then she did her incantation and before our eyes, Liam went from a lynx to a man about the same age as Gary with similar messy brown hair.

I forced a smile. "Okay. So now that we have that settled—what's the plan?"

"Ah, yes," Janice said, turning to me. "But first, let's eat." Then her eyes went to the bottle on the table. "I'll put *that* in a safe place for now."

I nodded in agreement. We wouldn't be pouring acid on Janice tonight.

The Long Goodbye

"IF YOU ONLY NEED me, another witch, to make the plan work, why didn't you and Gertrude do this long ago?" I asked.

We'd just finished the stew and bread Janice had manifested in mere minutes from the raw ingredients. Someday, I hoped I had the same magical prowess that she did.

"They built the city with emeralds and magic meant to bind spirits and curtail my sister's and my magic. You have changed everything, Dorothy. You are a witch not of this world, so it is doubtful the emeralds will protect them from you. With this," Janice stood and went to the counter, lifting the bottle of melting potion, "...we have some protection from Glenda, and it could buy us time to properly bind them and retrieve the soul of Oz."

"I thought you said we needed to kill them," I said.

Janice's eyes softened. "I did say that in anger, didn't I? I think we can effectively bind them without harming them—if things go according to plan."

The bottle made me nervous. "I don't want to kill anyone."

Janice set the bottle back down on the counter, then came over to me and gave my shoulder a reassuring squeeze. "I promise. I will not ask *you* to kill anyone."

The way she said it, it felt like the calm before a storm. You knew what was coming, knew it was inevitable, and felt helpless to stop it. I nodded. "Okay."

"I also suggest we find a way for you to get back home. I'm concerned the shoes may not be enough by themselves to transport you back to your own world. You'll have to somehow recreate the same conditions that brought you here to begin with, and maybe the Land of Oz has some magic of its own to lend." She smiled at me, and I smiled back.

Jason, Gary, and Liam had been quiet, probably grateful that they no longer had to be involved in the war of the witches. "We will look after Toto while you're gone," Jason told me.

Liam was the most fearful. Still a coward, but with good reason. "What if you aren't able to stop them and you both perish? What then?"

Janice sat back down at the table. "Then stay here and live out your lives as long as you can. The magic of this place shouldn't fade for hundreds of years. I've collected as much of the herb as I could in the past two days and planted the seeds all around the perimeter of this sacred space."

"That's grim," I said, the realization that I might never see Mark, my family, or my friends ever again hitting me like a brick in the chest. They'd all simply think Toto and I died in the tornado. An overwhelming melancholy overtook me.

"We have to try," Janice said. "Too many have died and suffered at the hands of *the Wizard* and his *sidepiece*."

There appeared to be a history between Glenda and Janice, but I didn't want to be nosey. I knew how complicated the battles between women could be. A lifelong rivalry could arise from an offhanded comment, one being bullied by the other, or a fight over a man. You just never knew, and right now, I didn't care. I just wanted to do what I could to help, and then grab Toto and get the hell out of Oz.

Gary had other ideas though. He'd chosen a weird time to finally find interest in others. "What is it between you two?"

"Who?" Janice asked, feigning ignorance. I could tell she knew who he was talking about by the way she tried so hard to appear unbothered.

"You and Glenda." Gary grabbed another slice of brown bread from the tray on the table and began munching on it.

I caught Jason cringe from the corner of my eye, but Janice didn't even flinch.

Instead, she forced an obviously fake smile. "Oh, you mean aside from planning the takeover of Oz all along? I'm pretty sure she's been the one whispering in Herman's ear. He wasn't smart enough to do all of this on his own. And people think *she's* the good witch. Ha!"

I nodded. "Yeah, that's the impression I got, too. That she was the one in charge, and he was just doing as he was told."

Janice pointed at me as if I was the validation she needed. "Exactly."

"Well, perhaps we should clean up," I said.

The men jumped up and went straight to work.

"Let's let them clean the kitchen. We'll go over the plan to get into the palace in the Emerald City, bind Glenda and Herman, and steal the soul of Oz. We also need to help you get home afterwards." She patted the back of my hand.

We retired to the living room as the men cleaned the kitchen. I pulled my grimoire from my bag, and Janice summoned hers. I couldn't help but feel impressed by her magical acumen.

"I can't wait until I'm that skilled," I said.

"You'll get there," she assured me. "You'll have to learn quickly if we're to succeed tomorrow. Now, let's look for things to get you home. Then we'll go over our trip to the Emerald City and all the magic needed there."

We spent hours going over the plan and poring over my grimoire and hers, exchanging recipes and spells as we went. By the time we all settled down to sleep for the night, we had a plan to bind Glenda and Herman, a plan to release Oz's spirit, and a plan to get me home. Glenda had even given me some herbs that I could use to recreate the veil-parting potion I would need to get back. The silver slippers with ruby chips were mine to keep as a gift from Janice for my help. They were part of Oz's magic that would give me and Toto the extra power we needed to get home. But first, we needed to survive the Emerald City.

There we were, inside the palace, but no one was there. Just me and Janice. Toto was there, too. Ankle-deep poppies concealed the floor.

"It's a trap!" Janice cried out. Then, from above, a water line must have broken because a spray of liquid poured over Janice. Her eyes widened with horror, and she reached out to me. "Dorothy, help me! Help me! I'm melting!"

As she became liquid, her face turned a slight green color, but then dissolved into a splash on the floor. Toto barked. A strange smoke filled the air then, and I found myself woozy. My vision blurred, and the room spun around me. The last thing I remember was falling into the bed of poppies.

Toto shoved his wet muzzle against my mouth and licked the side of my face.

"Stop it, crazy dog." Through sleep-filled eyes, I could see out the window from where I lay on the floor. The sun was shining, and the sky was blue. It was a beautiful day. I wondered if I had any orders. *What a crazy dream*, I thought, stretching my arms. Then the world came into view, and I found myself sitting in Janice's cottage. The men were still asleep, but I heard the clank of silver against ceramic. Letting my eyes adjust, I saw the slender form of Janice in the kitchen making tea. Throwing the blue blanket from me, I got up and looked out the window to the clearing surrounding the cottage. In the daylight, it looked like something from a fairy tale. Rabbits, deer, and even a horse grazed on the grass. A goat helped itself from a trough of water. I didn't see it, but I was pretty sure I heard a cow lowing. Janice hadn't lied. All the creatures of Oz had found a home here, in this magical, protected place, safe from the darkness of the spirit of Oz, and the malevolent couple in the Emerald City.

First things first, I needed to take Toto out, and I needed to freshen up a bit. When I returned, I found the table set with breakfast and the men just waking up. Janice provided another meal for Toto, and I sat down while she poured me a cup of tea. "Did you sleep well?"

I shook my head. My stomach was fluttering with nervousness. "Nightmares all night long."

"It's just the fear and uncertainty. We went over the spells last night, but should we go over them again before we go?" Janice sat back down.

"Yes, please." I wasn't sure I could do the spells she wanted me to do.

"It will shatter the emeralds, so head down and covered. Once that happens, I'll do the binding. However, if the emeralds don't shatter, you'll have to do the binding," she reminded me.

I nodded.

"You must believe you can do it, just like you believed you could ride out a storm and survive." She nodded and took a sip of her tea.

"Intent," I said, realizing Janice was right. While doing my protection spell during the tornado, I'd be lying if the image of a quiet, blue-sky paradise hadn't entered my mind. The desire to be anywhere but there.

"Yes."

The men finally joined us, and we ate our breakfast. When we finished, Janice used magic to clear the table and clean the kitchen. Then we went over the spells again. There were five of them. The first was to deal with any guards by turning them, temporarily, to stone. The second was to crush the emeralds to sand, thus removing the protections so Janice could use her magic. The third was to bind Glenda and Herman. The fourth was to shield Janice and me if necessary, in a bubble. The fifth was how to send bolts of energy from my hands to kill my opponent if need be. The last two were supposed to be last-resort measures. Janice also had, as a backup, the bottle of acid that Glenda had given us to use on her. I would go in first and distract them both, destroy the Emerald City and bring it crashing to the ground, and then Janice would be right behind me to do the binding. We'd have one another's backs.

Finally, Janice peered out the window to the sundial just outside the kitchen window. "It's time."

"Don't feed him too much and don't let him chase the other animals," I told Liam, charged with Toto's care while I was away. If I didn't return, he'd become Toto's new companion. *We're not going to fail*, I told myself. I gave Toto another kiss on the forehead and a quick neck rub. "Be a good boy," I said.

Janice forced a hopeful smile and gave me a sideways glance. "Are you ready for this?"

"As ready as I'll ever be," I said with a nod. Then I visualized the inside of the palace in the Emerald City—that shiny green throne room with the polished floors. With a deep breath, I clicked my heels together three times.

Oz Returns

THE WORLD SHIFTED SIDEWAYS and twisted slightly. Around me, the throne room shimmered into existence. But it was spinning, and I fell to my knees for a minute, balancing myself with my hands until everything wasn't so shaky. The room was empty, and I was facing the single throne. To my right was the side table that held the spirit of Oz. Janice would be right behind me, but first I needed to destroy the protection magic that kept her out.

"You can do this," I whispered to myself. Standing ever so slowly, I looked around, closed my eyes and began the spell to shatter the emeralds. I bent my head forward to shield my face, then I visualized the emeralds pulverizing beneath the power of the spell, turning them to powder. There was a sharp sound, not like a crash, but rather a crunch that had the same effect as nails on a chalkboard. I covered my ears and continued the chant, feeling the air around me fill with particles. Opening my eyes, I saw sparkling light all around me, and I pulled my shirt up to cover my nose, so I didn't breathe it in. Then, I waited for the emerald powder to settle.

There was a whoosh beside me, and I jumped, turning toward it. It was only Janice, who immediately spun around. "Well done, Dorothy," she said. "Are we alone?"

I nodded. "Not sure for how long though." The entire palace was now open to the elements. Shouts filled the air. Walking across the powdered emeralds, I went to the side table and the urn holding the spirit of Oz. The copper urn was vibrating ever so slightly. I picked it up, and it quivered in my hands.

At that moment, there was a loud crack and a puff of white smoke that slowly filled the space between Janice and me. Glenda and Herman stepped out of the wispy cloud, and when they did, the fog dissipated.

"Deceiver and traitor," Glenda spat at me.

"Sneaky, manipulative bitch," I said back, realizing that the Land of Oz's lack of dogs may have rendered the term *bitch* ineffective as an insult.

"This is the end, Glenda," Janice said. "The people of Oz will no longer live under your rule."

Glenda's eyes narrowed. Herman just stood there like a puppet, waiting for his strings to be pulled.

I steeled myself for the spell I knew was coming. Instead, Glenda said to Herman, "Get the fledgling witch. I'll deal with the *real* one."

It took me a moment to register the insult and her command, and by the time I realized what was going on, Herman tackled me, and I fell backward, the urn flying out of my hands and bouncing off the marbled floor. I'd completely forgotten the binding spell.

I didn't have time to see what Janice and Glenda were doing, only to save myself. I wriggled out of Herman's grasp and somehow elbowed him in the jaw in the process. It gave me a few seconds to scramble back to my feet.

He shook off the blow, but I could tell he was pissed. "How dare you defy the Wizard."

Unbidden, a laugh tumbled from the back of my throat because in my mind, that was something a teenaged LARPer would say. No one said stuff like that in real life. Not in Kansas anyway.

He lunged at me again, and I jumped back, my eyes darting to the urn, which I now realized had broken. *Damn it.* As Herman came for me, I cast the bubble spell. As he hit it, his face smooshed against it, and he fell backward. Not enough to fall on his ass, but enough that he had to shake himself off to realize what had happened.

Janice didn't seem to fare any better. Glenda had turned the emerald dust into spikes and sent them flying at Janice, who stopped them midair and crushed them back into dust. Without my help, it seemed doubtful we were going to win this fight.

Herman swung at my bubble as if trying to break it, but it didn't budge. His fists pressed into it, but they couldn't break through. I improvised. As he strained against the protection bubble, I let it down, and he fell to the ground. I put the bubble around him. Herman was the least dangerous of the two, and if I could occupy him long enough to keep him out of the way, I could help Janice with Glenda. Then we could deal with him. In his bubble, Herman shouted at me, but I couldn't hear him. The bubble had effectively blocked the sound of his voice. It was kind of funny watching him rage inside the clear sphere. Once I was sure he couldn't get out, I turned to Janice and Glenda just in time to see Janice douse Glenda with the liquid from the bottle that Glenda and Herman had charged me with.

"Is this what you were going to do to me? You have left the people of Oz lacking in leaders and drowning in crime," Janice screamed. "You murdered Oz and brought plagues on the land!"

Meanwhile, Glenda's moan escalated into a piercing scream. She seemed to be shrinking. Dripping. No, melting, I realized in horror. Glenda reached her hand out. "Why have you done this to me? I'm melting!" Then the sound of her cries faded, and all that was left was a puddle of water and goo.

"What the actual fuck?!" Slack jawed, I stared at the floor.

"Melting potion," Janice said, but by the tone of her voice, I could tell she was just as shocked as I was.

There was a loud pop, and both Janice and I turned toward the noise. The Great Wizard of Oz, Herman, had gotten out of his bubble. "You killed her," he said, running to the puddle on the floor and kneeling next to it, careful not to touch the goo.

Janice rolled her eyes. "Where's the urn?"

I pointed to the broken pot on the ground, and Janice let out a slight gasp. Her eyes traveled the room. "Oz?" she asked.

"Shit, did he get out?" I began searching the room, too, because if Oz had completely decimated the entire northern hemisphere of the Land of Oz, we were in trouble.

"Oz?" Janice repeated.

"Well, he's not going to answer you," I mumbled. "He's free now."

Herman stood and faced us, but there was something wrong. Where before there was fear and concern, now there was nothing. Even his eyes looked different. I thought I could see just a hint of crimson in them.

"Oz?" I asked.

Janice's eyes turned to me, and her face twisted into sheer terror. "Oh no."

"Oh yes, Janice, my dear witch sister." A slow smile spread over his lips. "And who is this enchanting creature?" His eyes saw through me, into the very depths of my soul. There was nothing human in that malevolence. "Ah, Dorothy Gale, from *Kan-sas,*" he said.

I swallowed the lump forming in my throat.

"I will need a new consort to help me rule the land," he said, and then I felt my body move toward him, as if being pulled by some unseen force. Pressure covered my entire being and my skin itched. Next thing I knew, I was wearing a strange silver gown to match my silvery red slippers. My hair was no longer trapped in the ponytail I kept it in. Instead, it fell loosely over my shoulders.

"No, Oz, you can't do this. It was wrong that Herman murdered you, but you have a choice. You can move on from this world and find peace in the next. I will make sure your legacy lives on," Janice pleaded.

I'd never heard her talk so fast in the entire twenty-four hours—less actually—that I'd known her.

"Go back to your cottage, Janice. Mind your business until I need you." With the flick of his wrist, Janice vanished.

"Did you kill her?" The sound of the terror in my voice chilled me to my core.

"Of course not," Oz said, in Herman's voice. Oz had possessed Herman and now owned his body. Herman had been nothing but a weak man under the spell of a powerful witch. With Glenda now dead, Herman had no one to protect him. We'd done this—Janice and I—unleashed Oz back to the land from whence he came, and that he had vowed to destroy. "You will become my consort, and we will rule this land with vigor and might."

No, no we won't, my mind screamed. "Will you restore the northern land and bring peace and prosperity back to the people?" I asked, taking care not to be overly emotional. Like a wounded animal, I didn't want to show any weakness.

His eyes bore into mine, turning even more red. He glowered at me. "Why can I not possess you?"

I shrugged. "Is that part of the plan?"

"What powers have you?" The question felt rhetorical.

"I make potions," I said. "I sell them to people."

This seemed to confuse him for a moment. "You are not a witch of this world."

"No," I admitted. "I am from another world, brought here by a magical accident, and I just want to take my dog and go home." I felt guilty saying it because it meant Janice would be left here to deal with an unhinged spirit possessing a weak-willed man in a power struggle for Oz and the life of everyone who lived here.

"You'll be going nowhere, young witch. For I need a bride and a child to carry on my legacy." Oz's mouth twisted with cruel glee.

Suddenly, a shimmering portal burst open beside me, and out stepped Janice and Toto. Toto ran out from behind her, approaching the wizard, barking furiously. This caused Oz to momentarily lose focus, probably wondering what the hell the creature was.

Janice wasted no time and cast a blinding flash of light, disorienting Oz. My heart raced as I seized the moment to knock Oz down. Whether it was reality or illusion, the remaining palace walls seemed to close in, and shadows danced ominously all around us. My breaths came quick and shallow, and I wasn't sure what to do next.

"Go, Dorothy!" Janice shouted, her voice cutting through the chaos. "Take Toto and find your way home! I'll handle him!"

I grabbed Toto up in my arms, not even deterred by how heavy he was, and visualized the house, but in my mind's eye I saw it on the grassy knoll. I clicked my heels three times before I realized I should have visualized the interior of the house itself, as it would have saved time. With one final glance back before we vanished from the palace, I saw Janice standing her ground, magic crackling around her as she prepared to face Oz. I heard a sickening snap, then there was a jolt, and Toto and I were left standing on the yellow cobblestone road, our house straight ahead on the grassy knoll.

There was a rustle in the hedgerow to the right and that's when Pornstache and his friends appeared. But there was something strange about them. Almost zombie-like. Even from the distance we were at,

I could see something wasn't right because their eyes glinted with crimson. They weren't moving fast, but I knew they were coming for me.

Something inside me screamed—run! I began running, calling to Toto. "Come on, boy! Come on, Toto."

He followed, and we ran. The munchkin zombie horde appeared to shift direction. Somehow, Oz had possessed all of them. Odd and unsettling, the throng of munchkins lurched and shuffled toward us with an awkward gait, their arms dangling unnaturally at their sides. Their sunken crimson eyes empty of any empathy or humanity stared into nothingness. Their mouths hung open, drool spilling down their chins. From their throats rose a cacophony of guttural groans that made the hair on my arms stand on end and despite their strange comportment, they moved at a surprising pace. Luckily, we were faster.

We made it to the house. Sprinting up the rickety steps, we rushed inside.

Next Stop, Kansas

I LOCKED THE DOOR behind us and began chanting the protection spell. It echoed through my small, battered house. Toto let out a howl, as if trying to add his own voice to the spell's power.

The ward took, spreading a brilliant violet light around and under the house, leaving behind the sickly sweet scent of the rotting corpse beneath it. That was a plus.

From the road, I could hear the angry crowd of Munchkins. There was nothing I could do for them now. I could barely make out what they were saying, but it sounded like, "Kill the witch!" How many people could this spirit actually possess at once? Apparently, many.

In my head, I once again imagined the villagers with torches and pitchforks. Toto whimpered at the door, but stood guard. I pulled my grimoire and the herbs Janice had given me from my pack and ran to the kitchen. With trembling hands, I opened my grimoire on the counter and shuffled around the mess to find additional ingredients for the potion. I mixed the herbs together, then threw in some bottled water. Fire conjured by magic had to be used to heat it. In a low voice, I began chanting the portal spell, visualizing my small plot of land in Kansas.

The voices were closer now. Then the banging came. The loud banging as they hit and clawed at the side of the house, trying to get in. But I focused with all my might, visualizing the house lifting into the sky, straight through the portal and straight back to Kansas. I clicked my heels three times. The floor beneath me jerked unnaturally, and I lost my balance. Toto made his way toward me, sliding along the wood floor until he reached me. I held out my hands and pulled him close. I continued to chant the spell just as the pot with the potion fell to the floor and splashed everywhere.

But the clawing and yelling had stopped, and all I could hear outside was the roaring wind that sounded like a train passing at high speed. Then there was a jolt, and Toto and I hurled toward the wall. My shoulder caught the brunt of it and all I heard from Toto was a yelp. Then came another jolt and the sound of wood splintering all around us. Finally, I felt the drop and my stomach jumped into my throat. My hands found Toto, and I held my dog and prayed to Hecate that we would make it out alive. I began reciting the protection spell again. One final jolt, and the last thing I remembered was my head hitting the wall.

I woke to the sound of Toto barking, and I opened my eyes. "Shit," I muttered. Then I heard voices. The hair on my arms rose. Any second now, the army of zombies would be inside.

"Get the door. Smash it open!" someone yelled.

Toto kept barking.

I tried to sit up, but only managed to roll onto my back. Everything hurt and everything, including me, was wet. Above me, I saw blue sky. The roof of the house was gone.

There was a crash as the door splintered open. "Dorothy?!"

I didn't have any fight left in me. It was at that point I resigned myself to my fate and closed my eyes. But Toto had stopped barking.

"Good dog," a man said. That voice was familiar.

I opened my eyes and tried to turn my head.

"Rory!" It was definitely Mark. He and my closest friends and family were the only ones who called me that. There he was, kneeling beside me and taking my hand in his. "Oh shit, we need an ambulance."

Relief washed over me, and I started laughing, but it hurt too much to laugh.

"I'll call emergency services," someone said.

"Why didn't you go to the storm shelter?" he asked. I could see the worry in his eyes.

I tried to speak, but my throat was too dry.

"You're alive," he said, holding my hand and rocking back on his heels. "You're safe now."

I wasn't worried about myself. I only hoped that Jason, Gary, Liam, and Janice had exorcised Oz and send him to the spirit world for his final rest. Hopefully, it was enough to save Oz from being turned into zombies, and to keep the land from dying.

After a short time, I remember hearing the ambulance and police sirens.

Mark glanced at me in the passenger seat. Toto, who'd only suffered a few already healed cuts from the entire incident, sat in the extra cab. His tongue hung out of his mouth as he excitedly watched the world pass by the truck window.

"You're not going to believe how much we got done," he told me, a hint of pride in his voice. He'd gotten a fresh buzz cut and I could smell a hint of musk in the air, probably from his soap.

I hadn't been back to the wreckage of the house since the ambulance took me away. Toto had stayed with friends who had a fenced yard, and I'd spent two weeks in the hospital and two more with Mark. My right arm was still in a cast. The neck brace had come off a week ago. "Did you take pictures for the insurance?"

He nodded, his brown eyes hidden behind his sunglasses. "Do you want to see them?"

I shook my head and turned my head toward the window to watch the cornfields go by. I couldn't tell Mark what had happened, but I knew it had, because in my belongings were the silvery red slippers. I'd kept them, if only as a reminder that I had been to the Land of Oz and had part of its magic with me.

"A lot of people were surprised you survived," he said. He'd been saying that over and over again for the past four weeks, almost like he couldn't believe it himself.

I let out a heavy sigh. I didn't need the constant reminder that I'd almost died, but I knew that repeating it somehow helped him with his own trauma of finding me inside the house.

"The new foundation has a built-in storm shelter," he said. Another thing he'd told me more than a few times. "Also, it's only a one percent chance a tornado will strike in the same place twice. I mean, how long did your Aunt Em live there? Sixty—some—odd years? And the house withstood all that time."

I gave him a weak smile. "Yeah."

"How are your arm and shoulder feeling?"

"They're good," I said, trying to muster some enthusiasm for the cleanup and the new house. Truthfully though, I was miserable. I didn't want Toto to have to stay with friends for months on end while we waited for the new house to go up. I didn't want to be stuck in an apartment in Topeka either.

"I have a surprise for you, though." He flashed me a big smile.

"I can't wait," I said, with far less enthusiasm than I meant.

We turned onto the road leading to the house. As we pulled up to where the house used to be, there were eight pickups of various makes, models, and colors parked alongside a big RV, the kind people took long vacations in. There were men working on the foundation of the new house, but there was nothing where Aunt Em's house had once stood. It was now a patch of dirt. The barn was still up, and I could still see the doors to the outdoor root cellar. The tornado had touched neither of them. My stomach did a somersault.

"It really is all gone," I said.

Mark parked the truck and turned off the ignition. "They took the last of what was left yesterday. It really is a surprise you survived it."

I got out of the truck, and Toto followed. Together, we walked to where the steps to the old house's porch used to start. Not even a splinter of wood remained.

It was bittersweet really, and the foundation of our new house was in full swing and looked amazing. A flicker of hope jumped inside me.

"Rory!" Mark called from the barn. "Over here."

I followed him into the barn with Toto at my heels. Mark motioned to a row of tables upon which a lot of my things sat.

"I was able to save some of it," he said with a hint of hope. "Any clothes we could save and wash, we did. But hey, new wardrobe for you, right?"

This time, I truly smiled and chuckled softly. "The two best things out of this entire experience. Shopping and starting our house sooner than we planned." Then I spotted a book. My grimoire! I hurried to it and picked it up, pulling it to my chest. Then I opened it. Despite the water touching its pages, the ink had not run, which surprised me. "I can copy it to a new book," I said.

But then, something else caught my eye. Something silver, gleaming from beneath a couple of purses. I pulled the bags away and felt the air leave my lungs. The silvery red stilettos. "Where did you find these?" I asked.

Mark came up alongside me. "They were outside the house along with a lot of other things, but they were still in good shape, so I thought you might want them. Though, if we're being honest, they're not really your style, babe."

"They're not mine," I said. My voice sounded small and even a bit terrified. "Was there anything inside them?" I asked, silently adding, *like feet or whole legs?*

"No, but some animal must have been crushed by the house because they were right next to it. Just a mass of rotting..." he stopped himself. "You get the picture. So I washed them and they didn't seem to keep the smell, so..."

"I want to burn them," I said as my eyes traveled over the tables, trying to identify any more remnants of Oz that had made the journey home with us. The idea that part of Gertrude had come back with the house made me sick to my stomach.

"What did you do with the dead lump of... whatever it was?" I asked.

"Picked it up with a shovel, threw it in a garbage bag, and tossed it into the dumpster," he said. "Why? Should I have buried it?"

I shook my head. "No."

It was better that he'd gotten rid of what was left of her. If he'd buried her, it would have been a constant reminder of my ordeal in another world, and the ground would have felt tainted with sadness somehow. At the same time, it seemed wrong that part of Gertrude would end up in a dump somewhere. *She left her body behind,* I reassured myself. But I didn't dare tell Mark that. I reached out and picked up the shoes by the heels.

"You really want to burn them?"

I nodded. "Yes. We should do it now."

With a shrug, he nodded. "Okay." He rummaged through the garage and produced a cauldron-shaped fire pit that had, at one point, sat between the house and the root cellar. Then he collected some wood from the back of his truck and some lighter fluid from inside the RV. After a few minutes, the little cauldron fire pit had a blazing fire in it, and I tossed the shoes into the flames, saying a silent spell to send Gertrude on her way and to send her silver slippers to her in the afterlife. Stepping back to avoid the acrid smoke that emerged, I could almost taste the magic of the Land of Oz.

"You must really hate those shoes." He gave me a quizzical look.

"I'll tell you about it sometime. It's not important now." I motioned toward the RV. "So, what's this?"

"Oh, this is the surprise!" He motioned toward it like a game show model presenting a new car. "This is now our home away from home. At least until the house is built. That way, Toto can stay with you." Then he moved around the RV and pointed to a new pole on the corner of the property. "You now have your own tornado siren."

"How did you..."

"I know a guy," he said. Then he took off his sunglasses. In the sunlight, his brown eyes looked almost bronze and earthy. "You still have a storm shelter. I mean, just in case you are really unlucky and the RV gets swept away to..." He didn't finish the sentence.

"Swept away to where?" I asked. Something inside me churned, but I pushed it down. Way down. I was being ridiculous. It's not like part of Oz the spirit could have survived the journey and jumped into Mark. Mark wasn't behaving weirdly. He wasn't trying to harm me, turn the builders into zombies, or take me back to his land—the Land of Oz.

Mark just shook his head. "The next county over?"

A part of me sighed in relief. "Let's check out the RV then," I said. We went inside.

Outside, Toto looked around and planned his next move. He didn't know why he was here in this foreign place. He only knew it was Dorothy who had set him free. He remembered possessing Herman, and that he'd been cast out by the only living witch in Oz—Janice. He'd made it into the Munchkins, had almost gotten to Dorothy. For reasons he didn't remember, he knew he wanted her. Wanted to possess her and own her. He'd been able to jump into the strange beast he now inhabited, just before it got inside and went through the portal. Now, he could get revenge. On whom—he didn't remember. The clearest memory he had was of Dorothy, and how she was to be his consort. A mild wind caressed the beast's nose. The air here smelled different. Spreading his magic feelers, he could tell that this land was bigger and had fewer witches as strong as Janice, Gertrude, and Glenda. Slowly, he would turn Dorothy to his side. She would come to love him. He would have her. As her beloved pet, it would be easy. As her betrothed, it would be easier, but he had to wait to move from the beast to the man. There was time. No one would ever see the great spirit of Oz rising from the Kansas crop fields to rule this world. However, it was time to rest, gain strength, plan, and play the part of a witch's familiar—for now.

Twisted Tales of Familiar Faces

If you enjoyed this corrupted retelling of *Alice in Wonderland*, don't miss out on the rest of this horrifying collection!

Humbug (Scrooge) - Andre Gonzalez

Sweethaven (Popeye) - RJ Clark

Timber Beast (Paul Bunyan) - A.K. Hughey

Alice (Alice in Wonderland) - Audrey Brice

Wish (Aladdin) - Courtney Konstantin

Quixote (Don Quixote) - Stephen Wertzbaugher

Arturius (King Arthur) - A.K. Hughey

Steamboat (Steamboat Willie) - Courtney Konstantin

Strangled (Rapunzel) - Stephen Wertzbaugher

Dethroning Oz (Wizard of Oz) - Audrey Brice

Scorned (Hercules) - Z.S. Diamanti

Check out the entire collection at www.m4lpublishing.com

Join our newsletter to stay up to date with all upcoming releases at www.m4lpublishing.com

Author's Note

Thanks to M4L Publishing and Andre and Natasha for inviting me to participate in this project, and for working so diligently to bring it to life. You both are amazing.

Enjoy this book?

We hope you enjoyed this release from M4L Publishing.

Reviews are the most helpful tools in getting new readers for any books. We don't have the financial backing of a New York publishing house and can't afford to blast our books on billboards or bus stops.

(Not yet!)

That said, your honest review can go a long way in helping us reach new readers. If you've enjoyed this book, we'd be forever grateful if you could spend a couple minutes leaving it a review (it can be as short as you like) on the site you purchased this book from.

Thank you so much!

About the author

Audrey Brice writes award-winning dark fantasy, paranormal, urban fantasy, supernatural horror, and mystery novels. She also writes under three different pen names including Anne O'Connell, S. J. Reisner, and S. Connolly.

www.ingramcontent.com/pod-product-compliance
Lightning Source LLC
Chambersburg PA
CBHW030906200726
48289CB00003B/917